'A most plausible and authentic-sounding novel, and one which I heartily recommend.'

Coventry Evening Telegraph

'The final chapter . . . is one of the best pieces of sustained dramatic writing I have read since the climax of Nigel Balchin's *The Small Back Room*.'

Huddersfield Daily Examiner

'A thoroughly professional writer. His characters are neatly introduced and described. His dialogue, like his plot, is crisp and convincing.'

Argosy Magazine

WARREN TUTE was born in County Durham and educated at the Dragon School, Oxford, and Wrekin College. He entered the Navy in 1932 and retired in 1946 after a career which included service on Earl Mountbatten's staff and a part in the North African, Sicilian and Normandy landings. After the war he wrote for films, radio and television. He has travelled widely, especially in America and Eastern Europe. Apart from plays, film-scripts and historical books, he has written ten other novels including *The Cruiser*, *The Rock*, *Leviathan*, and *The Admiral*. He is married with two children.

WARREN TUTE

A MATTER OF DIPLOMACY

UNABRIDGED

PAN BOOKS LTD : LONDON

First published 1969 by J. M. Dent & Sons Ltd.
This edition published 1971 by Pan Books Ltd,
33 Tothill Street, London, S.W.1

ISBN 0 330 02623 2

Printed and Bound in England by
Hazell Watson & Viney Ltd,
Aylesbury, Bucks

The characters and the situations depicted in this book are entirely imaginary and no resemblance to living persons, and especially to any past or present members of the British Embassy in Athens, is intended.

I

As the aircraft gained height Elissa began to relax. So far so good. She had forgotten how pleasant it was to travel first class even with this new temporary identity the Foreign Office had given her and the children. How long would that small protection of her privacy last? The Greeks were restlessly, incessantly curious. They were born intriguers, and gossip, as she well knew, was the small change of Athens. She gazed out on the white cloudbanks below with that hard suspicious glance she was so accustomed to giving the world and which when she looked in the mirror she so much wanted to lose. She would be grateful for even three days of privacy and freedom from curiosity.

The steward asked her if she would like something to drink, and she ordered a dry martini for herself and Coca-Cola for Mark and Lucy. They were alone in the first class. She wondered if Marides had fixed it that way. It was his airline. This could all be part of his extraordinary, quixotic gesture. She had little doubt she would find out what he really wanted when they were installed in the villa. Conceivably it could be nothing. Marides was internationally rich enough to indulge in disinterested generosity. Or did any such thing exist in the world today?

'What did you say, Mummy?' Lucy was asking.

'Nothing. I must have been thinking aloud.'

'You often talk aloud to yourself.' Mark leant back from the seat in front. 'Didn't you know?'

She stared coolly back at her son and smiled at his gravity. He looked so like his father, even to the intensity in the eyes.

'That comes of living alone,' she said.

'But you don't live alone,' Lucy chipped in; 'there's us. We live with you.'

'She means because Father left us. Anyone knows that.'

'Mark, don't always put Lucy in her place. She's just as clever as you are.'

'She's two years younger and she can't even read yet.'

'Mark, remember what I said. This is just how I don't want you to behave. We're all going to have a holiday by the sea for the first time in three years. We've all got to try and make it a success.'

'Why do we have different names on our passports?'

Instinctively Elissa looked to see if the steward could overhear. Perhaps anyway he was in the know.

'We've been through all that. So that reporters and photographers won't bother us – we hope.'

'It's because of Father, isn't it?'

'Of course!' Elissa snapped impatiently. 'Of course it's because of Father. I don't want it mentioned again. This is supposed to be a holiday for me as well.'

The captain came through in a cloud of after-shave lotion and the glinting charm of the Greek in uniform.

'Everything all right, Mrs – Mathews?'

The momentary hesitation told Elissa all she wanted to know. They were still specimens under the microscope. She managed a frosty smile.

'Thank you very much.'

'No doubt someone from the British Embassy will be there to meet you.'

'I hope not. Anything not to attract attention from the *papparazzi*.'

'The *papparazzi* are Rome, Mrs Mathews. We order things differently in Greece. We Greeks know how to respect privacy. The state of affairs at Rome airport would never be tolerated in Athens.'

He gave her the benefit of one of his veiled, condescending glances. The day of the travelling British milord was over, it seemed to say. You may be a friend of Mr Marides but you are in a Greek aircraft, captained by an officer of the Air Force reserve. He treated her to a dazzling smile, patted Mark on the head and made his entrance into the Tourist Section where his uniform could be assured of greater impact and respect.

'This is our flying house,' said Lucy, walking round the compartment like a cat as soon as he had gone. 'Just for us three and no one else.'

'I wish we were going to see Father,' Mark said, not looking at his mother.

'You know that's not possible, so what's the point of hankering for things you can't have?'

But the sullen look had come back into his face. 'I only said I wish ...' he muttered, turning his back on his mother and sister.

The captain was right and they had no unwanted attention at Athens airport. They were quickly and authoritatively passed through Customs, and as they were about to go out into the hard sunlight, a young man with an agreeable smile quietly took charge.

'The car is just round to the right.' He flicked his fingers at the porter who had evidently been briefed before. 'Welcome to Greece.'

'Are you from the Embassy?' Elissa asked.

'Not the British Embassy. My name is Jean-Pierre Mournier. I'm a fellow house guest at the Marides'. Panayotis is away in Crete but he should be back in the evening. He asked me to take care of you and make you feel at home.'

He spoke excellent English with a French accent, taking Lucy by the hand and guiding Elissa firmly to the Rolls-Royce with the waiting chauffeur. Mark was very impressed with the car. The sulky resentment had gone and he was again the man of the family taking charge of his mother and sister. Mournier saw this and played up to it, giving Elissa a rather shy little smile as if she were being made party to a secret.

'He's very like his father, isn't he?' Mournier said when Mark was out of hearing.

'Did you know Paul?'

'I've seen photographs.' There was no penetrating that sophisticated charm which left so much unsaid.

'Which embassy are you from?'

'I'm on holiday too, like you. But you know Greece well, don't you, Mrs Tarnham?'

'Oughtn't you to go on using our cover names? After all, I have a passport saying I'm Mrs Joan Mathews. The Foreign Office was surprisingly helpful.'

They were travelling along the coast past Vouliagmeni towards the Marides' estate.

'The chauffeur doesn't speak English and Panayotis is in on the act – isn't that how one puts it?'

She sat in silence, vaguely annoyed at the way this stranger seemed to know all about her affairs within five minutes of meeting. But Marides had to be trusted. She supposed this young man had been told what was necessary and no more. The events of the last three years had taught her never to volunteer information of any kind. She accepted a cigarette and gave him a smile. 'I can't really believe we're back in Greece. Paul and I did two years here when we first got married, before the children were born. Do you know Greece well, Mr Mournier?'

'Jean-Pierre – please. No, this is only my second visit. It's a little different from Switzerland. But then they say Greece, like Paris, is a state of mind. It's a pliant country. Whatever you want is here if you look for it.'

'All I want is the sea and the sun and a little peace.'

He smiled faintly and pointed out a landmark to the children. Elissa lapsed into silence. The blue sea and the clear, clear air were already beginning to work their old spell. Already, as she was half afraid would happen, her wariness was becoming lulled. She remembered with a touch of irritation Paul's saying that, however critical you were of the Greeks, their country was irresistible. What did he mean by pliant? What in fact was this urbane young man doing in Marides'

Rolls-Royce as if he part owned it? She found him looking at her as she turned her head.

'There's nothing sinister about me,' he said. 'I happen to be a friend of Marides' son – the one in the Greek Foreign Office. So you really must do as Panayotis says and relax. You are among friends.'

The villa was large without being ostentatious. It was superbly sited with a view of the Aegean which no travel brochure could beat. Both Mark and Lucy were given rooms of their own, although Lucy said she intended to sleep with her mother. The privacy afforded by the house and estate could only have been purchased in that part of Greece by a millionaire, and this was but one of five or six houses which Panayotis Marides maintained in different parts of the world. There was a secluded beach and a little island within swimming distance offshore. The children had never seen anything like it before, and the contrast with the shabby Fulham apartment they had left earlier that day could not have been greater. The marble floors, the Renoirs, the white-coated staff – the whole *ambiance* made a numbing impact, and although Lucy was really too little to understand, Mark asked:

'Why has Mr Marides asked us here?'

'He's your godfather, Mark.'

'I know that. Does he want to marry you, Mummy?'

'Good heavens, no! To begin with I'm married already.'

'You know what I mean.'

He was eight years old and she did know what he meant.

'Mr Marides is a very rich and generous man. I think he was as fond of your father as he was of me. He just wants to give us a nice time.'

'Like nobody else in England.'

'Yes, Mark, as we've all found out in three years.'

'Because of what Father did.'

'Mark, will you please not talk like that! Put on your sandals and we'll go and explore the beach. Jean-Pierre says there are buckets and spades in the beach hut. And I'm going to swim.'

Panayotis Marides had been born in a poor village of the Pindus mountains. From there he had gone to Cyprus, and from that springboard had dived into the rich waters of world shipping, becoming yet another Greek myth in his lifetime. He was a realist not much given to philanthropy. As he grew richer he greatly enjoyed the exercise of power. He joked and laughed a lot, but he was not what the English call 'a nice man'. He was something of a bully, and his values, in spite of the yacht and two art collections, were those of a peasant whose real respect is for money.

'People who say money doesn't matter usually don't have very much,' he was fond of saying. 'I have a great deal and I know that it does.'

'Then what are you doing asking church mice like us to sup at your table?' Elissa asked that evening when they were alone together on the terrace for a few minutes.

'If you played poker, my dear, and knew the other players in the game, which you do, you wouldn't ask a silly question like that. In any case you can guess the answer to that one, so why bother to ask? Unless, of course, you're just playing for time. Now I've arranged a small programme of entertainment for you and the children, for Jean-Pierre, and for the Germans and Americans who are arriving tomorrow.'

'I just want to lie in the sun and do nothing.'

'You'll have plenty of time for that too. I think the children should see Delphi, don't you? And you might like to consult the oracle yourself. On Sunday – by the way, Helen's coming from Paris on Saturday – we shall be organizing our archaeological picnics.'

'I thought you and Helen were separated.'

'We're divorced. It was cheaper that way. But she still comes and stays when she wants to, as she always did. Surely you've learnt by now that sex and marriage have nothing in common?'

He put an arm round her shoulders and made the invitation a little more obvious.

'You don't just pay for your women with a good dinner, do you? I thought you were more subtle than that.'

'It's a question of response, isn't it?' He gave her a knowing smile. 'There are always other ways of getting what you want. And other things to want. All I want for the present is to make sure your holiday is a success. Nothing else.'

'I believe you,' she said and kissed him as he wanted to be kissed. She was quite capable of keeping him guessing too. For good measure she told him that Lucy would be sleeping in her bed that night. This made him laugh.

'Are you sure you don't play poker?' he asked and kissed her again.

'There's one little chore I have to do tomorrow,' she remarked as she broke away, 'and that is call on the Ambassador. The Foreign Office made a point of it.'

'You'd better do it in the morning then. The Ambassador's going to London on the afternoon plane, leaving Rupert Eynsham in charge.'

'Ah yes, Rupert Eynsham,' she said and looked at the lights of Athens twinkling in the distance. 'How strange to be meeting him again out here. Is Claudia still with him?'

'You seem to specialize in asking questions to which you know the answer.'

'Well, is she?'

'Claudia is one of the jewels in our Athenian diplomatic diadem. She and Helen get on so well together. They have a common interest in archaeology. And God knows Greece has enough ruins to keep them happy. But you haven't come here for the ruins, have you?'

'No,' she agreed, 'I haven't come here for the ruins.'

II

THE British Foreign Service is not usually ostentatious in the accommodation it provides for its diplomats abroad, and the Counsellor's private residence in Kyfyssia was no exception to this unexceptionable rule. But it did have a garden. Every morning when Rupert Eynsham woke up he could see the garden and took pleasure in the bougainvillea and flamboyants which seemed almost to hurl back at him the early morning sunlight. This battle against the ants and Mediterranean horticultural hazards which Claudia had at least partially won in the garden was a stroke in her favour, Rupert reflected. At least she got some satisfaction out of that – that and the dog she was determined they would take back to England and put through the quarantine process. But was that all she really had to show for her life?

He looked at her plain beaky face on the pillow and wondered how he had ever thought her attractive enough to marry. Or she him, if it came to that. Now that he was in his greying fifties she must see him as a slightly paunchy, tame – or rather tamed – disappointment of a man who had neither succeeded nor completely failed in his career, for whom there was still hope, but to a yearly diminishing degree, and for which she blamed one man and one event, the defection of Paul Tarnham. But then Claudia was a great one for blaming anyone other than herself for what went wrong in her life.

However, today, he thought, as he got up and shaved, today was D-day. 'D' for disposal. That little runt of an Ambassador would be winging his pawky way to London for a week, and Claudia too would be bound for Mykonos where she was going to sail with some brigadier cousin of hers who seemed to have done rather better out of commerce than the Army, and whose snobbishness Rupert found unbearable. Claudia admired that kind of success, fancied him as a man and enjoyed his company. And the best of British luck to you both, thought Rupert, humming to his image in the mirror for the first time in months. He wondered if they had ever made it together and, visualizing that possibility, actually laughed aloud. The rorty brigadier must have a taste for lean stringy meat, though of course she had been a baronet's daughter and that made up for a lot.

'Rupert, I've been thinking,' said Claudia as he returned to the bedroom and began dressing, 'I really don't think I can go sailing with Arthur – not at a time like this – with the Ambassador away and you on your own.'

Steady there, fellah, don't panic. She's done this before. Give her plenty of rope, salve her conscience, don't appear too eager and she'll talk herself back to it by breakfast.

'Well, you're the best judge of that. There's nothing on the calendar of earth-shattering importance. I mean, you won't be missing anything in the great diplomatic world of Athens for the next week or ten days. But please yourself. If you feel you must stay, Claudia, light of my life, then stay you must. You know your responsibilities to Her Majesty's Foreign Service and to this bastion of bureaucracy better than I do. It'll be great to have you around.'

'You're so cynical, Rupert – why do you sneer all the time?'

'But I don't. That's what passes with me as a joke.'

'Anything I do, anything I suggest, you send up. I get so bored with that so-called polished irony you affect. I don't find it funny at all.'

Here beginneth the nagging for the day, he said to himself. Speed up the dressing, old chap, and slither away to what that bloody Greek maid imagines is toast and coffee. She'll come round, once she's up on her two spindly legs; she really longs to go sailing with Arthur, but she also wants to be Mrs Acting Ambassador while the going's good and terrorize the Embassy staff. Well, she can't have it both ways and no doubt we'll soon have an embassy of our own. Any day now I shall be getting that private word from Stevens in London. Can't be much longer now.

'I think you just want to be rid of me,' Claudia went on when she joined him at breakfast. 'That's the impression I get.'

'I wish you'd get rid of Eudoxia or whatever her name is and find someone who can boil water and pour it over coffee grounds without making it taste like swill.'

'I sometimes wonder if you're not having an affair with your secretary. You can't wait to get to your desk and she obviously dotes on you.'

'It's a nice idea. I'll give it some thought.'

'These debby brats they send out now: they're not even efficient. Look at the hash she makes of running the Embassy library.'

'I thought that was your job. You volunteered as far as I knew. You always get first pick at the book of the month.'

'Your beloved Janet is supposed to assist me. After all, she works in the Embassy and I don't. I've never known a girl get a simple matter like issuing library books in such a first-class mess. She'll end up by putting everyone's back up – just see if she doesn't.'

'Well, I must be on my way. Let me know if you're going sailing with Arthur or not. He'll feel a bit let down if you don't – and I much doubt if you can get a message through in time. But that's up to you.'

He pecked her on the cheek, picked up his briefcase and made for the car. Outside the early summer day was intoxicating with its brilliance and clarity. He was always glad to get out of the house and there were simple compensations like the weather there for enjoyment, if only you were aware. He paused for a moment before starting the car. A bird sang and the sunlight poured steadily down. Soon he would be in the clatter of Athens, immersed in another day. The bird continued to warble away – or was it Arthur's mating call from Mykonos? And would Claudia hear it in time?

At the British Embassy the great engine of bureaucracy – England's only remaining export to Greece, according to Eynsham – had already been started, and was comfortably idling in a Monday morning way. Trim, thin Anglo-Saxon secretaries had opened the offices and sorted the mail, arranged the flowers and discussed their weekends in preparation for the arrival of the Ambassador, his second in command, the Counsellor, and other important principal officers of the mission.

Janet Mortimer was twenty-one and this was her first tour of duty abroad. Already in a couple of months she had brought a new look into Rupert Eynsham's affairs. The second lady of the Embassy might call her a 'debby brat', but Claudia overlooked the fact, which Rupert certainly did not, that Janet could do the chores of the job – the dictation, the typing and the filing – with an ease and speed which would have got her a better salary in business than she was ever likely to get in government service. She was aware of this too, but even today, as she told the military attaché, money was not everything. She wished he wouldn't drop in for a chat at such odd times and ask such chatty little questions. 'You see, Father was an admiral, the background was right and we're all prisoners of convention when we start out, aren't we, Major Axley?'

'What's this Major Axley kick? I was Stephen yesterday.'

'Yesterday was Sunday and we were climbing Hymettus. Today is Monday – this is the British Embassy and I'm giving a more formal look to the week. Or is the military attaché only passing the time of day?'

'No, Janet, as a matter of fact I wanted to have a word with you before the Counsellor gets in.'

He looked at her blue eyes and short dark hair, he considered her very desirable body, and he wondered how the hell he could put it and whether she would play ball. It had kept him awake half the night. Delicate diplomatic approaches to secretaries in key positions had not been on the curriculum at Sandhurst, and this was one of the many occasions when Axley wished he had never taken up intelligence work but had stuck to simple soldiering.

'Go ahead. He'll be in any time now.'

'Yes. Thank you – I don't quite know how to begin.'

'You certainly weren't diffident yesterday. What's the trouble?'

'No trouble. It's just that it has to do with the Counsellor.'

She glanced at him warily and then continued to sort out the file on her desk. 'Oh yes! What?'

'Well – you know about the Tarnham affair, don't you?'

'Doesn't everyone?'

'Did you realize that when Tarnham defected, Rupert Eynsham was head of Tarnham's department in the Foreign Office? He was his immediate chief.'

'He was cleared at the inquiry.'

'Completely.'

'But he's still being watched? It's over three years ago now.'

Axley's discomfort grew. It had been a mistake to rely on the old boy net. He should have sent for her in his office and done it officially. 'Well, we don't have guys in black capes and sombreros following people round Athens,' he said unhappily, 'but of course, in view of the circumstances of that very exceptional case—'

'I thought Tarnham took nothing with him – no codes or ciphers or what have you. Surely he wasn't a traitor in the accepted sense, was he? The public inquiry settled that, didn't it? He just simply left the office one evening and instead of going home fetched up in Moscow. Isn't that what happened?'

'No one officially knows where he is. He hasn't been identified like Philby or Maclean. He may even be dead.'

'But there's still a blight on Mr Eynsham?'

'I wouldn't put it that way. As you pointed out, he was absolutely cleared at the inquiry. But he and Tarnham had been friends as well as colleagues. And it certainly hasn't helped his career. He should have been an ambassador years ago.'

'What's all this leading up to?' There was a slight edge to her voice.

'You know what my job is here in this Embassy, don't you?'

'You're the Security Officer. Our very own James Bond and all that.'

'On certain delicate matters I report direct to the Ambassador.'

'And this is delicate?'

'Yes.'

She gave him a cool look. 'I'm afraid I won't spy on my boss, if that's what you mean.'

'That's putting it far too bluntly. You wouldn't be asked to and certainly not like this. No, Janet, I have a small piece of news and I want your help, that's all. The news is that Elissa Tarnham – and her two children – are here in Athens. All I want to know is if she tries to get in touch with the Counsellor – that's all.'

'And you couldn't ask him yourself?'

Axley frowned. 'Don't make such a song and dance about a very simple request, or am I to tell the Ambassador I'm not getting the cooperation I need?'

Now she was angry. 'You can tell the Ambassador anything you like. And I'll let Mr Eynsham know about the pressure you're putting on me behind his back. I'm not an informer. And never will be.'

She looked marvellous now her temper was aroused. Axley recovered his poise.

'Oh, come off it, sweetie. This isn't blackmail. It's a perfectly ordinary request made in the line of duty, that's all. See you for dinner tonight.'

'And I wouldn't rely on that either.'

At that moment Eynsham came into the room.

''Morning, Janet – 'morning, Stephen.' He looked with mild and somewhat impatient curiosity at both of them, vaguely aware of the tension, his mind on the tedium ahead.

'Have you anything for me, Stephen?' He went on: 'I've got to get the Ambassador off to London.'

'No, it was just the report on General Toroporides, but that can take its turn.'

'All right then, let it wait.' He smiled in dismissal and Axley left the room. 'Now then, Janet, what's in the mail? Anything personal for me from Stevens?'

'Not in that lot. It may come in the noon delivery.'

Briefly she ran over what there was in order of importance. Already, for reasons he didn't bother to analyse, he felt a disquiet. 'D' for doom, not disposal, he thought illogically as he flicked through his 'In' basket. Perhaps there was thunder in the air. He looked up through the french windows at the Embassy garden with its beautifully tended lawn. Heaven knows, there were causes enough. Getting the little man to the airport, getting Claudia away, no news about his promotion, still the shadow of the Tarnham affair – surely by now he was free of that? He could feel the habitual unease building up like a headache. By doubt out of uncertainty, he thought, one reaches ulcerdom, that limbo land on the road to despair.

'Are you all right?' he heard Janet asking anxiously. 'Can I get you something to drink, or an aspirin?'

She was a sweet girl. Why did he not have a daughter like that? Where had it all gone wrong? He shook his head and gave her a smile.

'Just a touch of the Monday morning, I think. Have you got my wife's ticket for Mykonos?'

'It's on the right of your desk.'

'She may not be going after all. But don't cancel it until she tells you definitely herself.'

'H.E. would like to see you with the Turco-Bulgarian trade pact file – oh, and that report on Markopoulos and his Communist son.'

The birdsong at Kyfyssia was already another life. It would all be better when he was on his own. Loneliness be my friend, he said to himself. It will all be better when that plane takes off for London. A good part of his uneasiness was his dislike of and contempt for the little bureaucrat who was his immediate superior. It was irksome that his fate still lay so much in James Harborough's hands. He would have to steel himself to ask a favour of the pompous hypocrite. He would have to ask him to find out from Stevens at the Foreign Office what was still holding up his promotion. Even Guatemala on his own would be preferable to being number two in Athens. He picked up the files and went into the Ambassador's room.

Major Axley was with the Ambassador. When Eynsham came into the room they stopped speaking abruptly in such a way that it was obvious they must have been talking about him. James Harborough gave Eynsham a bleak smile and a nod of dismissal to his military attaché.

'Ah, there you are, Rupert.' He said it as if he had been waiting half the morning. 'Now I've one or two things I must turn over to you before I go. Frankly I really don't wish to be away at a time like this.' Meaning, thought Eynsham, that the last person you want to trust and leave in charge of your Embassy is me. 'Don't think for a moment, my dear Rupert, that I don't realize you'll run things, in my absence, very much better than I do. I've every confidence in your ability. It's simply that with the border tension and the present state of the régime, I'd rather be keeping my fingers on the pulse of things here than jabbering away in conference at the Foreign Office. However, orders are orders.'

'Things are very quiet at the present.'

'I don't think I'd put it quite that way, but of course I respect your opinion.'

'At any rate I can't see anything to panic about. Naturally, the moment you go all hell will break loose, but I rather doubt it.'

Eynsham suspected that Harborough enjoyed the cut and thrust of thinly disguised insult as much as he did. It spiced

'I don't care to bring the word panic into our discussions, Rupert, even in fun. There are more than enough delicate their daily work.

problems to keep us awake at night without the necessity of being flippant.'

Why did the little man dislike him so much? Of course he was still Mr James Harborough and not Sir James; but as this was his last appointment before retiring no doubt a grateful government would reward him with his K in the end. He couldn't blame the delay on the Eynsham appointment. It couldn't be jealousy, because what was there to be jealous about in himself? It was more likely to be fear. But fear of what? That some of the scandal would break over their heads? Undoubtedly that was what it had been in the early days after the inquiry when Eynsham had been appointed to Athens to get him out of the way. The smear of the Tarnham affair had not been a welcoming factor in his relationship with the five-foot-five Ambassador.

'I'll be frank with you, Rupert,' he had said at their first meeting. 'I'm delighted your name was completely cleared, but of course there's always a residue of doubt left in people's minds. It's always unfair and it's much worse for you than it is for me. But you're bound to continue to attract interest and curiosity. We shall have to devise ways of setting people's minds at rest.'

'Like keeping our mouths shut,' Eynsham had said bitterly, and that had begun the feud. Even now, nearly three years after the event, when neither had won nor could possibly win, the effects of the smear were still poisoning their relationship.

'I wonder if you'd have a word with Stevens if you've time?' Eynsham said. 'I really do need a change of air. I'm overdue for a post of my own. And surely by now the Tarnham affair must have worked itself into – well, into being a non-factor at least.'

'I would have thought so, Rupert,' the Ambassador said with relish, making it clear he was suddenly weighing his words. 'But unfortunately the very opposite has happened. For reasons I simply cannot fathom the FO have given Mrs Tarnham assistance to come out here under a false name with her two children to stay with Panayotis Marides

– ostensibly for a holiday in the sun. It's extraordinary – and as I was telling Axley just now – by the way he knows all about it – there must of course be an ulterior motive. Of course *there* we're not to be let into the secret.' The habitual sneering bitterness had returned to the voice. 'So, as always, the people on the spot are left to grope away in the dark.'

'Perhaps there isn't an ulterior motive.'

The Ambassador stared at him as if he were a candidate for a job who had made a particularly unfortunate remark. 'Isn't that being a little disingenuous? When we don't even know if Tarnham is alive, let alone where he is?'

'You think he might be here in Greece?'

'I think this may be a trap. For a number of people.'

'But Marides plays ball, doesn't he? He's a British subject.'

'He's a Greek shipowner. With whom he plays ball, why and when is your guess as well as mine. Trust is another matter entirely.'

There was a pause while both men explored their own thoughts. Eynsham could well understand why Harborough had no wish to be summoned to London at a time like this.

'Mrs Tarnham was a friend of yours, wasn't she?'

'They both were – as the inquiry exhaustively showed.' The Ambassador had flinched at the word.

'Hm!' There was another pause in which the mutual dislike built up. 'I think, if you'll accept a piece of advice,' he went on, 'I'd keep away from the lady here in Athens. It's a complication we can all do without.'

'Yes,' said Eynsham; 'with that I agree.'

Back in his own office he found Claudia bullying his secretary about the way library books were issued. She always did this when really confused, always on a busy morning, always attracting the most attention.

'I came in to cancel my tickets but Miss Mortimer tells me it is too late.'

'Too late to get a refund, that's all.'

'Why don't you go as arranged?' Rupert said, thinking of Elissa and the possible complications ahead. 'I'll be perfectly all right. Nothing's likely to happen.' Nothing that a small nuclear bomb wouldn't cure.

'Well ... if you really think it's all right?'

'And you won't be letting down Arthur.'

'I shall feel so guilty – leaving you all alone. Still, you have Miss Mortimer to take care of you.'

'I expect you'll get over it,' Rupert said lightly. 'The feeling of guilt, I mean.'

'Very well then, I'll go. Can I borrow Miss Mortimer for a moment or so? The library is in a terrible mess.'

He avoided Janet's imploring look.

'All right – but only for five minutes. We really are busy this morning. H.E. should be at the airport in just over an hour.'

When they had gone he sat down at his desk and stared once more at the green Embassy lawn. It was laughable really how you couldn't win. Three years ago his world had fallen apart because of Paul Tarnham. And here it was back again ... He remembered how his own father had been in the zone for promotion to commander – that crucial step in a naval career – in the autumn of 1931. Suddenly out of the blue the Invergordon mutiny had involved him in a disaster on another scale and had swept away his career, as the Tarnham affair had dashed Rupert's chances of an embassy of his own. *Plus ça change* ... but why? And now, when it was reasonable to suppose that time had healed the damage which timing had done, here – here in Athens – was Elissa Tarnham and all that she threatened. Certainly there was a trap – but for whom?

The telephone on Janet's desk had been ringing and now there was a knock on the door.

'Come in,' Rupert said without turning round. He was lost in an old familiar reverie compounded of doubt and acceptance, of sensing his fate and of puzzlement at the unexpected events which twisted it into a new direction. Why then was a fresh possibility always accompanied by this deep sounding sense of doom? Of course he was in Greece, and the Greeks with their hierarchy of tragic gods were really first in the field with that kind of philosophy. Come now, Eynsham, he told himself, stop elevating your rotten little career to the level of Zeus.

'Hallo, Rupert,' said a very familiar voice. He turned in his chair and looked at Elissa. For a moment neither said anything at all, she looking at his troubled face, he trying to control his emotions.

'Hallo, Elissa.'

'Surprised?'

'Shattered.' She made his heart leap but he could not get a welcome into his voice. His diplomatic training had automatically come into play so that there was no visible reaction at all.

'But you knew I was coming?'

'I'd be the last person to hear the news.'

The cool grey-green eyes, the slim boyish figure, the small breasts and the wide cheekbones – he could see no change from the years ago. How could Tarnham have left a woman like that?

'By the way, I'm supposed to be Mrs Joan Mathews. The Foreign Office gave me a passport in another name.'

'They must be getting very skittish these days back in the Whitehall branch.'

'I'm here with Mark and Lucy for a holiday, Rupert – just that and nothing more.'

There was a trace of acid in the voice.

'So why come to the Embassy?'

'To call on the Ambassador as directed by the Foreign Office. You think I enjoy it?'

'I wouldn't know about that.'

He was once more aware of that instant rage which before had made her personality so tricky and unpredictable. He noticed it still brought a colour to her cheeks. He had forgotten details like that in three years, but now it was all coming back.

'I thought you'd be surprised, Rupert. I wasn't prepared for this glacial reception.'

'Did you fancy I'd throw myself in your arms?'

'I don't expect anything these days, and that's rather an unfair remark.'

She was as wary as a cat in danger.

'I don't think fairness comes into it.'

'Then you must have changed a lot.'

A somewhat flustered Major Axley appeared. 'Excuse me, sir, I just heard that Mrs – Mathews was with you ...'

'Did you, Stephen?' He turned to Elissa. 'You'd better meet this one – this is Major Axley, our military attaché – he seems to know all about it.'

They shook hands.

'How is it, Stephen,' Eynsham went on, 'that I had no warning of Mrs Mathews's arrival?'

'I don't know, sir. I suppose it was an Ambassador-only telegram.'

'The Ambassador and you.'

'Well, sir, it's—'

'It's the job – yes, I know. However, I think someone might have dropped me a hint.' He was becoming coldly angry as this new slight to his authority sank in.

'Shall I take her to the Ambassador, sir?'

'Thank you, Stephen, I can just manage to do that myself.'

The door opened and Claudia and Janet came in. Janet seemed to be on the point of explosive tears. Claudia was exhibiting the satisfied look of a suburban matron who has caught her domestic stealing the groceries. The change when she saw Elissa almost made Rupert laugh out loud.

'Good heavens above, Elissa, what are you doing here?'

'This is *Joan Mathews*, Claudia.' Rupert stepped in quickly, compelling her attention. 'Do you understand? She's here under a different name to avoid publicity.'

'How quaint! I should have thought it would achieve exactly the opposite result.'

'You could be right at that,' Elissa remarked.

'Where are you staying? At the Grande Bretagne?'

'She'd hardly stay at the most famous, most central hotel

in Athens if she wanted to avoid attention, Claudia, now would she?'

Claudia produced her schoolgirl trill which for thirty-odd years had covered up her nervousness and private fears.

'There you are,' she said, 'you can see I haven't changed.'

'I'm staying with the Marides.'

'Good heavens! How did you manage that?'

'I was asked.'

'Such an insufferable little man! Of course, I suppose if you're all that wealthy, you must also have the vulgarity to show off whenever you can.'

'I thought you were friends with his wife?'

'I'm sorry for poor Helen, if you want to know. But don't let's waste time on the Marides. How long are you going to be here?'

'Three weeks or a month. It rather depends ...'

'Then you must come and dine with us when I get back.'

'You're off sailing, are you?'

'Yes, but only for a week.'

How did Elissa know that? Rupert wondered in passing and made a slightly impatient sign at his wife.

'You'll miss your boat if you don't go now.'

There was always enough to do in the office without any visitors at all.

Claudia extended a chilly smile, allowed Janet to walk across the room, put the tickets in her hand, open the door for her, and then like the Edwardian *grande dame* she wished she could have been, made her exit. Rupert caught Elissa's eye with a flicker of understanding and quickly jumped in.

'Come along. I'll take you in now. I suppose you'd better come too, Stephen.'

By the time they reached the Ambassador, Rupert was seething with anger. He was still tainted, still under suspicion. Three years of blight and nothing had changed. He glanced with mounting distaste and dislike at Elissa. She was the cause of it all. He watched her bow stiffly to the Ambassador. The little man had stood up but had not come round from behind his desk and did not shake hands. Brief formalities were exchanged, then the Ambassador came straight to the point.

'Now, Mrs Tarnham, as I think you know, the Foreign Office has asked me to keep an eye on you here during your visit to Greece.'

'No, I didn't know. I was told to call on you, that's all.'

'You didn't expect to be under surveillance?'

He spoke with asperity as if to a junior clerk.

'That would be too much to hope for.' Elissa had no trouble in matching his tone and Rupert saw the inevitable clash suddenly on top of them. 'However, I thought the idea behind giving me a passport and special facilities in another name was to avoid publicity and possibly allow us to have a holiday undisturbed.'

'No doubt you did, Mrs Tarnham.' He managed to inject so much acid contempt into the name that even Rupert was surprised. His own anger began to give way to a sort of sympathy for Elissa. This too, he instinctively realized, was dangerous.

'No doubt you did. However, what the Foreign Office do in London is one thing, what I do here in Athens as ambassador is another. It's not for me to query why you were allowed to come here at all, but you are here—'

'You know, I find your tone of voice extraordinary, Ambassador.' Elissa's eyes were like the North Sea in a winter storm. 'Whatever my husband did or did not do, I myself – and my children – are perfectly innocent and ordinary citizens. We're free. We've done nothing wrong. I'm not on your staff. I don't have to obey your orders, nor do I have to put up with your vile bad manners. Good morning to you.'

Rupert was delighted to see that the little man had been momentarily stunned into silence. Elissa turned away and began to make for the door.

'I'm afraid it's not quite as easy as that, Mrs Tarnham. On the passport you hold you are to a certain extent under my orders ...'

She continued to the door without turning round and

abruptly left. The three men looked at one another for a moment.

'Go and head her off, Stephen, and ask her to wait in my office,' Rupert said to Axley, who quickly followed her out.

'Well ...' said the Ambassador, 'I've never been spoken to like that in my life – and in my own Embassy! What a nerve – from a shabby little traitor's wife.'

Pick up the pieces. Pat it all back into place. Round and round goes the wheel.

'She was always a woman of spirit,' he said.

'No wonder Tarnham left her.'

'She's been under considerable stress for three years.'

The Ambassador gave one of his affronted terrier looks. 'I'm well aware of the facts, thank you, Rupert. I can dispense with the special pleading.'

'Yes, but it *was* rather a frosty welcome, Ambassador.'

He could almost see the terrier bristling.

'And what was I supposed to do? Go down on my knees and kowtow?'

'Of course not. However, she is, as she said, an innocent victim of it all.'

'Yes,' said the Ambassador, giving him a long, steady look. 'Perhaps – perhaps so far she is. Ask Axley to come and see me right away, will you? I'll be going in twenty minutes.'

III

THEY sat in a secluded corner of the Kalamaraki, a little restaurant overlooking the harbour of Piraeus. It was discreet, a place for anonymous lovers, the privacy guaranteed to a certain extent by the bill.

'I'm glad you could make it,' he said. 'It was nice of you to come.'

'Who else besides your secretary knows we are here?'

He shrugged his shoulders and stared out to sea. 'Does it really matter?' he said.

'You were the one who insisted on separate cars – and all that security nonsense.'

He ordered two more Ouzos and toyed with his glass. 'Wasn't it Somerset Maugham who said, "Do what you like but keep an eye on the policeman round the corner"? It's not a bad working rule. There's a limit to the idiocies they can impose on human behaviour.'

She looked so cool, somehow aquamarine and very desirable. He directed his mind away from that dangerous area of thought. His membership of the sexual playground had long expired.

'Yes,' she said gently, putting her hand over his, 'they've had far too good a run for their money with both of us these last three years. Why were you so angry at seeing me again this morning?'

'Fear, I suppose. Work it out for yourself.'

'Did you think I'd come all this way just to open it up again? Just to make trouble for you?'

He studied her face but she avoided his eyes. 'Why have you come?'

'I told you.' The sharpness was back in her voice. 'I wanted a break.'

'Why couldn't Marides invite you to one of his other Palazzos?'

'Ask him yourself.'

There in a few short sentences he had blown away the delicate mood. That pattern, too, was very familiar. The food came and they began eating in silence.

'You're very on edge, aren't you?' Rupert said eventually. 'You seem to be cool and controlled, but you're not. There's no need to be that way with me.'

'I'm sorry I snapped just now. I'm worried about Mark and Lucy if you want to know.'

'They'll be all right, won't they? Who's looking after them out at Marides' place?'

'A young Frenchman – at least I think he is – called Jean-Pierre Mournier. Mark likes to be independent, so he'll be all right. Lucy gets a bit fraught if I'm not around – but in any case I don't like having them out of my sight for too long.'

'You never used to be as nervous as that.'

'That's right, Rupert. Things were different in the garden of Eden.'

Gradually as the meal progressed he got her to relax. She had been interrogated so many times in the last three years that she now seemed to have an outer layer of evasiveness which he found irritating. He felt often as though he were talking to a mask with a hidden watchful being behind it. He had never liked actresses, and now he recognized the same double personality in this woman to whom three years ago he had begun to be drawn. He wondered if this watchfulness had been there all along, or if it was something acquired as a result of what had happened. She struck him now as more attractive than ever before. Again he consciously put that side of things out of his mind.

'And you still don't know where Paul is – nor even if he is alive?'

'Officials don't give a thing away. I've been up against a conspiracy of silence.'

He noted almost automatically that she rarely answered the question he asked, always deflected an interest which seemed to pry, always turned away the direct and probing inquiry.

'It may seem silly to you, but I can't stand people asking me questions. And that's all they ever do. For three years I've been a sort of fairground oddity. Roll up – roll up and see Tarnham's wife!'

'That's stretching it a bit, isn't it? I mean, after the initial shock.'

'You wouldn't say that if you were me. And you must have had it too.'

'Yes, to begin with. After all I was his boss.'

'But I was his wife – whom he left. That makes a Sunday paper curiosity. "Tell me, Mrs Tarnham, what were your feelings when you realized he'd gone? What's it like being left high and dry?" – What is it like? Lonely.' The hard suspicious look was back in the eyes.

He stared away at the busy harbour below and visualized how her life must have been. 'Incidentally, how have you got on for money?'

An earlier, funnier sardonic expression animated her face, and for a moment or so she looked like a girl. 'They don't pay defectors' wives very well. We didn't fit the regulations. Luckily my parents helped out and we got this roomy old flat in Fulham. But prising anything out of the state when there's a security hoo-ha on isn't funny at all. As Paul used to say, when the civil servants have got you by the short and curlies they can't resist paying off a few old jealousies and envies of their own. Like flaunting the advantages of behaving yourself and having a good steady job in times of crisis. They must patronize. One or two of them were sympathetic and kind, but the Establishment God is a severe old piece of constipated scabbiness. We all know that. He's not to be mocked. And Paul certainly did that.'

'Government service means and always has meant that hypocrisy is an occupational risk. Like the Church.'

Out in the harbour two caiques narrowly missed being rammed by a steamer and some frenetic hooting began and then ended abruptly. As if it were some sort of alarm clock, this set up in Rupert the uneasiness he had for a few moments forgotten. He paid the bill and Elissa went to the lavatory. On her return he saw a man get up from a table by the bar and speak to her. She listened for a moment and then shook her head.

'What was that all about?' he asked her casually as they made their way outside.

'He said would the Ambassador and I like a private car and guide for a trip to Delphi?'

'Oh, Christ!' said Rupert, and then as they got in the car: 'Did he know who you were?'

'I don't think so. He called me Mrs Mathews.'

'He knows,' Rupert said. 'The Greeks find everything out.'

Over the next few days Rupert felt a chemical change taking place inside him. He had forgotten what it was like to be in love. With Claudia away at home and the Ambassador gone from the office, the sudden freedom was at first heady and rejuvenating and then somewhat dangerous in the possibilities which began to leap to his mind.

The morning after Claudia had gone he sacked the maid after throwing her vile coffee down the drain. He paid her approximately half what she demanded, and sent her away muttering Greek threats which he knew would result in visits from relatives, possibly the police and even the burgling fraternity. He didn't care. He always had resented her smug inefficiency and the bland way she had held them to ransom because they were '*diplomatiki*'. He told Janet to find him another and get her installed before Claudia returned.

At the office he put a bomb under the routine and disposed of his own and everyone else's 'Pending' trays as much as he possibly could. Harborough was a great teeterer and talker. He liked to be sure. In practice this meant that nothing went through in one. Every file with a proposal for change went back at least once and sometimes a dozen times for quibbles to be settled and 'further consideration given'. Rupert changed all that.

'When the Ambassador does return,' Janet said to Axley, 'there won't be anything for him to do except take a few days' leave. Mr Eynsham's into his Churchillian syndrome and everything gets marked "Action this day".'

'I'm not sure what syndrome means.'

'Neither am I. But it sounds sort of Greek and nice.'

'You're really hooked on the Greeks, aren't you?'

'Some of them. And some of them get hooked on me.'

'Is that a boast or a threat?'

'Young Marides, for instance. He came to see the Counsellor yesterday afternoon and made a nice little pass at me. I thought you'd like to know. He's asked me out to his father's on Sunday.'

'Has he?' said Axley. 'And what about me?'

'Apparently there's some sort of archaeological picnic for the oldies and the speedboat and water-skiing for types like young Mr Marides and me. Mr Eynsham's asked too. But he can't go until after church. He says he'd have to attend church, as we can't let the old governesses down. I didn't know there were any left in Greece.'

'You should see them on the Queen's Birthday Garden Party. They come out of hiding once a year to take tea and cakes on the Embassy lawn. Of course it thins out a bit each year but there are still a few left.'

Axley perched on her desk – which privately annoyed her – and brought himself to ask the question she knew was coming.

'And how's it going with Elissa?'

'Ask him yourself.'

'Cooperative as ever.'

'Stephen, you know how it is. A spy is a spy is a spy. And I'm not.'

Axley made like the Kitchener recruiting poster. 'Your country needs you, Janet.'

'Does it? Would you get off my desk?' She looked at him pert and self-assured. 'Let's be honest for once. Do you think anyone really cares?'

'If you feel like that, we might as well all pack up and go home.'

'I thought that was what had been happening ever since the end of the war I missed by two years – everyone packing up the jolly old empire and going off home. Anyway the Counsellor isn't a Philby or a Donald Maclean.'

'How do you know?' said Axley, clattering out of the room. 'Paul Tarnham was.'

* * *

As the week went on neither Elissa nor Rupert made any attempt to get in touch with the other. She remained with her children out at the Marides' house. Rupert got on with the daily Embassy chores. This set his mind at rest in one direction and screwed him up in another. Had he made no impact on her as a male human being? Did she not feel anything for him as a man? Has Eynsham the great lover had it? he asked himself in the shaving mirror, uncomfortably aware of the basic sexual activity she aroused in him when he woke up from sleep. Perhaps he ought to invest in some new after-shave, buy a sports car, generally acquire that young masculine look which the girlie magazines suggested was what women went for these days in a man. It all seemed a little remote from the greying, soberly dressed English diplomat whose sexual fantasies were quickly put in their place by the morning mail. Yet not entirely submerged – having Janet around in the nearest to a mini-skirt she could get away with in the Embassy kept him constantly aware that he was still a man.

On the Thursday he rang her up at the Marides'. The moment he heard her voice at the other end of the line the sense of doom came thundering back so that he almost put down the phone straight away.

'How are things?'

'Fine. Two of the papers wanted little interviews, but they've been taken care of...'

The phrase coming out of the telephone had a chilling suggestion of gangsterdom about it. But this was a reaction which leapt to the mind these days when force worked so near to the surface of Greek affairs. A sinister interpretation could be put on the most innocent remark when there were dictators around.

'I wondered if we might risk a dinner.'

'Very diplomatically put. Which of us is taking the risk?'

'I've got some cultural do at the American Embassy this evening. I'll put in an appearance and then pick you up afterwards – around eight.'

'I don't like leaving the children.'

'Oh, come on, Elissa, things aren't as tricky as that.'

'They're my children, not yours.'

He could visualize the strained, anxious face at the other end. 'Well ...'

'All right, Rupert, I'll try. It's just that Lucy gets scared if I'm not around.'

He put the phone down and gazed out at the Embassy garden. British soil in an alien land, protected by all the ancient power and privilege, now somewhat on the wane but still as puissant as ever, so far as embassies were concerned. A castle of freedom in a land where those ideas were currently taking a beating – and there was Elissa outside in the cold, afraid her children might be abducted for some obscure political purpose. He shook his head. If he hadn't known Tarnham over the years, if he hadn't been fully and admiringly aware of Elissa's basic common sense, he would have explained away her fears as a bout of hysteria. But he had misjudged Tarnham completely, and now with Elissa he was beginning to feel very much at sea. On an impulse he sent for Axley to come and see him.

'If you can answer this question without offending any of your security dicta, perhaps you'd tell me if you think Mrs Tarnham is in any danger here in Greece?'

Axley at once looked uncomfortable. We put our security in the hands of the strangest and nicest young men, thought Eynsham, whom the other side must simply read like a book.

'Danger from what, sir?'

'You tell me. I mean, was it a mistake to come here with her children?'

'I really can't give an opinion on that, sir.'

'Can't, Stephen, or won't?'

He actually blushed. Eynsham smiled at his embarrassment. He knew that the young man liked and admired him, and had even admitted to Janet one day that he thought Eynsham was worth a hundred Harboroughs. He knew that Axley found this current situation highly distasteful.

'I'm not quite sure what you're asking, sir. I'm not stonewalling, but as Tarnham hasn't yet shown his hand in three years, I'd say there was always an element of danger to his wife and family. I mean, I wouldn't myself, if I was Mrs Tarnham, bring my children out here to Greece for a holiday – not under the present régime.'

'Thank you, Stephen.' The military attaché quite obviously knew more than he wanted to say. Eynsham pondered this disquieting thought for a moment or so.

'Was there anything else, sir?'

'I don't think so. I shall be taking the lady out to dinner tonight – to save you the trouble of finding out from other sources. I'm not quite sure where it will be – probably a *taverna* farther along the coast from the Marides'. But I'll be taking an Embassy car so you can check with the driver.'

'Are you implying that I spy on you, sir?' Axley said unhappily.

'Well, those are your orders, aren't they, Stephen? Let's not fool ourselves too much of the time. I'm still under the Tarnham cloud. You might as well give your masters a bone to bite on.'

'Excuse me for suggesting something, sir – but do you have to give Mrs – Mathews dinner tonight?'

A spasm of deep sudden fury gripped Eynsham so that he felt an actual pain in the solar plexus.

'Of course I do, Stephen.' He said with a thin smile: 'Even an acting ambassador has a private life. And there's not much fun in a sitting duck, is there? We all like a run for our money.'

As Axley left and Janet showed in the Turkish Ambassador, he wondered almost clinically where the seat of the danger actually lay. What and where was the threat he felt spinning in the air? He watched Janet's exciting little bottom disappear through the door and devoted his official self to Her Majesty's interests in Greece.

IV

JANET had fallen into the habit of taking an evening drink, often followed by dinner, with the military attaché. She was aware that Stephen Axley regarded this as mixed business and pleasure. He often got more out of her than she imagined, but whenever she realized this she told herself he had to do his job, and anyway she liked him. Behind the carefully built up, carefully controlled Sandhurst arrogance, she could see a rather shy and uncertain man, unduly sensitive to people but having to pretend to a brusque personality that was not really his own.

The first time he kissed her she had also found out he was married.

'But Fiona didn't like it in Delhi where we were before and she got tired of it here, so home she went together with the child. There's always Mummy, you see, and rather a lot of money.'

'Don't you love her any more?'

'Sort of. I mean, I miss her and I miss Susan a very great deal.'

'How old is she?'

'Just four.'

'Are you separating or getting divorced?'

'Oh, I don't know. We both keep putting it off. But I don't see how it can work. She always has to have her own way. What my mother calls headstrong.'

'And your mother likes her?'

'Can't stand the sight of her. Jolly little family it all adds up to, doesn't it?'

He had tried to kiss her again but she turned him away.

However, he proved to be persistent. The wooing had gone on from day to day, and although she had never been to bed with him, this was more because of the difficulties of embassy life and the fact that it would at once be known and noised about than for any particular scruple. At least this was the excuse she gave to herself for always putting him off.

That evening, as they sat in the Oasis Bar, he seemed more pensive than usual. She asked what was on his mind.

'I seem to have provoked a sort of declaration of war by your boss', he said, 'without in any way meaning to. And it's the last thing I wanted to do.' He told her about his suggestion to Eynsham not to take Elissa out to dinner that night.

'Well, it *was* rather cheek, wasn't it? Grandmother suck eggs and all that. I mean, why shouldn't he take out his old girlfriend when his wife's away? You do.'

'I just think it's not a very good idea.'

'But of course you can't say why. So the mystery image builds up – but where does that get any of us?'

'You know perfectly well, Janet, that I can't ever go into details. You'll just have to take it from me that as things are here today it's *not* a good idea.'

'And suppose the Counsellor doesn't agree? It's possible he knows just as much about intelligence work as you do and simply doesn't agree. He's no fool: he doesn't panic and he has had considerably more experience than you.'

Axley set his mouth grimly and put on his worried, preoccupied 'Secret Service' expression, as Janet had once called it to his face.

She laughed out loud. 'You really are screamsville, aren't you? The way you go on as if any of it mattered.'

'I'm not in the mood for that kind of frivolity.'

'All right, pomposity, drop me off at the flat.'

'I thought we were having dinner together?'

'Not if you're going to be like that.' He looked so downcast she went on quickly; 'Look, Stephen, Mr Eynsham is a sound, solid man – you've said so yourself. He knows what he's doing, probably better than you do. Why don't you relax about it all? He's a good man. He's not going to let anyone down.'

Axley stood up and picked up the bill. 'All right, Janet, I'll drop you off at the flat.'

Out at the Marides' Elissa was trying to deal with a tearful and frightened child.

'But you'll be asleep, Lucy.'

'I shan't.'

'And I'll only be out a couple of hours. There'll always be someone here. And Mark isn't frightened.' Why did she have to plead like this for a little time to herself?

'Mark's a boy. Besides, he's older than I am.'

Elissa looked at the tear-stained face reddened by the sun and the beach.

'Don't you want me to have a nice time too?'

Lucy did not answer, but looked at her hands. 'That's not fair,' she said. Where did children get this immediate, applicable sense of justice? 'Can't I come too?'

'No, of course you can't. It'll be hours past your bedtime. Look, shall I see if Jean-Pierre's going to be in tonight?'

'Don't care.' The little six-year-old bundle of misery knew she was not going to win, but it hurt Elissa to see the child retreating into herself. There were times when she found she could scarcely bear the loneliness of the human condition in general and her own and her children's in particular.

'Look, darling, if it matters all that much to you I won't go.'

'Don't care,' said Lucy, tearing a strand of hair from her doll, followed by another.

'Then I wish you wouldn't always sulk about it,' Elissa said in irritation and regretted it the moment after. 'I have a life as well, you know.'

She changed and went down to the drawing-room. Panayotis was again away on one of his trips, but his son was there talking to Jean-Pierre Mournier.

'I'm being taken out to dinner tonight,' she said, 'but I've had a little trouble from Lucy about it. Will you be in, Jean-Pierre?'

'Of course. I'll look in to see they're all right. Mark may want to go down to the beach and inspect his aquarium, but I'll tell him not tonight.'

'Good Lord, has he been down before?'

'Yes – for the last two nights, but it's a secret. You're not supposed to know. So don't give me away, will you?'

'No, no, I won't give you away,' she said, feeling the uneasiness well up in her again, 'although I don't think it's a good idea. You can give me another martini.' She stared back in a troubled way at young Christos Marides' dark Greek eyes as he gave her a cigarette. She was reminded of two sleek little cats licking their paws in the sunlight.

'I have another letter for you,' Christos said, bringing it out of his pocket, 'which I'm sure you'll be glad to get.'

The cultural reception was for the work of three young American painters. Normally Rupert found these exhibition launchings paralytically boring – in part because Claudia fancied herself on art and also because no real communication ever took place between the diplomatic and official guests and the unhappy progenitors of whatever artistic extrusion happened to be on view. They were failed non-events.

Tonight, however, Claudia was away. The tingle of danger he had felt since Axley's rather clumsy warning had tightened him up all round. He was no longer one hundred per cent a machine. The exercise of a little choice in the running of his life added a liveliness and relish even to yawners like this. Two of the painters were notorious homosexuals in the local scene, and the diplomatic element with similar tastes had flocked loyally to their aid. Unfortunately the work on view was nondescript to a degree so that very few people bothered with the pictures but quickly got on with the drinking.

His American counterpart, Dick Everitt, a Bostonian whom he liked and respected, sought him out and asked where Claudia had gone.

'Boating round the islands with an old boyfriend,' Rupert said.

'In the ambassadorial yacht?'

Rupert laughed. This was a reference to earlier days when the British Ambassador had set his heart on getting a yacht put at his disposal by the Foreign Office so that he could escape from his study at the Embassy when it was unbearably hot. Whitehall had noted the request for a yacht and the reasons therefor. To meet this requirement they had asked the Ministry of Works to supply an air conditioner for the Ambassador's study. This had become known throughout Athens as the British Ambassador's yacht.

'I hear that rogue Marides has an interesting house guest,' the American said, giving him a quick look.

'Yes,' Rupert countered without showing surprise, 'and an American citizen into the bargain.'

'What bargain? She was born in Minneapolis, that's all. When she married into your diplomatic service she had to renounce.'

'Well, Dick, the way things are today you might well find her unrenouncing again on your very own doorstep. I don't imagine she's been having too gay a time in England these last three years.'

The other made a great play of lighting a cigarette. 'I don't think she'd be very welcome if she tried that particular line. After all, Rupert, what man of wisdom consciously adds to his troubles?'

'Oh, there are always one or two hardy souls,' Rupert said. 'See you later, Dick.'

He had forgotten her American birth, he reflected, as the car took him out to the Marides' house. She had no trace of an accent, having left the States as a child. As far as he could remember her father was in some agricultural machinery business which had taken them about the world. He turned over in his mind for a few moments some of the possible permutations of citizenship as they could affect people's lives in awkward situations and began to grope his way into the future.

As his brain had been trained to do, he ran over the facts. He was in love with Elissa as, he now admitted to himself, he had been since their first meeting four years ago. Then Paul Tarnham had been an up and coming number two in Rupert's department at the Foreign Office. The two families had exchanged the normal hospitality, but since Claudia had taken an instant dislike to Elissa, their social encounters were purposely few. But the chemistry had gone to work. He could not get her out of his mind. She set him on fire without, so far as he knew, being aware of the effect she caused. He was sensitive to her vibrations. This was an accident of life, he knew, but none the less painful for having to be completely suppressed. She was not vibrating specifically at him. Alone on a desert isle she would still have been the same slender boyish-feminine woman with the high cheekbones and the Katharine Hepburn personality vibrating away to the bees and the flowers. She just happened to hit him plumb in the guts. For a time it had been an agreeably masochistic agony. Like Paul Tarnham himself, Rupert was basically an introspective brooder. He had always been low on sexual aggression. But it looked now as if he were going to have to sail against the wind of his nature, if this present chance, which instinctively he knew to be the last he would be given, was not to disappear in the blue.

'You've time for a martini, haven't you?' Christos Marides asked, after Rupert had been introduced to Jean-Pierre Mournier. He enjoyed exhibiting his father's wealth, particularly to threadbare British diplomats who in the popular view crept around Athens worrying about their allowances. Rupert noticed how Jean-Pierre Mournier immediately seemed to sink into the background, leaving the limelight to Christos Marides. He wondered if this was on purpose or if the young man had a natural shyness. Since the advent of the present régime, strangers meeting for the first time were more than ever wary of each other. Young Christos Marides, however, was body and soul for the new establishment. It was a rich soil in which to cultivate ambition.

'Of course you've been here many times before, haven't

you?' he said; 'but my father was hoping that you and Mrs Eynsham would honour us with your presence on Sunday. My mother is coming from Paris for an archaeological spree and, naturally, we hope to have other amusements for those with more mundane tastes. But Mrs Eynsham likes archaeology, doesn't she? And she will be back by Sunday?'

'I hope so,' Rupert said formally, wondering how the Marides knew that. He did not remember telling anyone else how long Claudia would be away. Of course it might simply be a bow at a venture.

'I don't want to leave Lucy for too long,' Elissa said, finishing her drink. 'So let's be on our way, Rupert.' Deftly she got them out of the house and into the car.

He had chosen a fairly simple *taverna* looking on to the sea where the lobsters were good, and the other clientele unremarkable. It was a warm, windless evening, ideal for the purposes he had in mind. By this time his nervous apprehension instead of being numbed by alcohol seemed to dry his throat and make him totally unrelaxed. Elissa, on the other hand, snuggled into her chair like a cat and exhibited no outer trace whatever of the anxiety about her children which was never far away from her mind. They exchanged one or two trivial remarks about the view and then Elissa triggered him off.

'You seem very jumpy tonight. Am I that difficult to take out to dinner?'

He smiled rather wanly. 'I don't know what it is about you, Elissa, but you make me feel like a gauche little boy. I really think you might help me a little.'

'My dear Rupert, in what way?'

'Oh, don't be so bloody arch! You weren't like that the night we all went to the Savoy after that ghastly Argentinian reception. The first time I ever held you in my arms.'

'In those days people didn't dance by themselves.'

'Well, it did it for me. That's when I became hooked.'

'Just over three years ago. What did we dance – the minuet?'

She was enjoying the embarrassment with which he picked his way through the minefield. She looked ravishing and he could have strangled her.

'Did Paul ever guess?'

She was tempted to say 'Guess what?' but decided this would be pushing it too far. Instead she took off the pressure a little.

'If he didn't, he'd have been remarkably thick. And Paul was never that.'

'Did he ever mention it to you?'

'You seem to forget, Rupert, he disappeared a few days after that evening.'

Once again she had evaded the direct questions he asked. For a while they said nothing. From a nearby house *bouzouki* music filtered on to the terrace of the *taverna.*

'Where is he?' Rupert suddenly asked.

'I don't know.'

'But he's still alive?'

'I don't know.' She was looking at her drink. 'I should imagine so, wouldn't you? They'd have no reason to dispose of him, don't you think?'

'And he's never been in touch with you since he went?'

'No.'

He wondered if she was lying. He found it strange that he could not immediately tell. He wanted her very much and yet he would never trust her. Or didn't trust her now. But then he was still in the middle of the minefield, probing a way ahead with only the most primitive detector there was – his own instinct and native wit.

'What are you going to do?' he asked eventually. 'You can't go on for ever like this.'

'I hope not. You have to experience limbo to know what it's like.'

'I know another part of it well – and like it as little as you do.'

'Yes, Rupert, I'm sure.' He was aware of a sudden concentrated look she was giving him. 'When is your promotion coming through?'

'That's one thing I've asked Harborough to find out if he can.'

'Is Stevens still there?'

'Yes, of course he is. Didn't you see him when they issued your passport, Mrs Mathews?'

She hesitated for a second before answering. 'No, I think he was on leave at the time.'

Now he knew she was lying. But why?

'You see, Rupert,' she suddenly said, 'I think they've really let me come here as a trap.'

'To catch whom?'

'Well, obviously Paul, of course. If he's still around.'

'And you let yourself be used as the bait?'

She sighed, looking as if she might burst into tears. 'I'm so tired of it all. He's still my husband, if he's alive. He's still the father of my children. They need him. I need him too.'

'Yes,' he said with a heavy heart, 'I know what you mean.'

V

As the meal wore on it seemed to Rupert that the same pattern he had come to recognize all through his life was again repeating itself. Mister Near Miss or Baron Second Best, the shaving mirror names he gave himself after nocturnal reflection, now once more made their shadowy appearances. Like death they waited for recognition.

'Do you still make up those awful clerihews?' Elissa asked.

'Like why does drinking Ouzo make me want to screw so? Yes, the old crossword-puzzle life goes on in the intervals of crises much as before.'

They went back over their previous meetings before the

Event. Both were beginning to relax and the food and the wine were helping the process. He found it was still possible to make her laugh. She in turn enchanted him and a slow fire began to rage in his veins.

'If I hadn't been sent here under a cloud, I'd have enjoyed Athens as she is there to be enjoyed,' he said, 'even with the Greeks around.'

'Paul and I loved it. We were sent here just after we got married. Those were the shaky days when a paper cost five thousand drachma and a meal ran you into millions. I think the Greeks rather miss those days.'

'The mentality hasn't changed, as you must have found from staying in Palazzo Marides.'

'Paul used to say the Greek character sat on a three-legged stool made up of charm, *philotimo* and a cheerful abandonment to almost total dishonesty.'

He began to be rather tired of hearing what Paul used to say. 'We have to be a little discreet about definitions of that kind today,' he said, 'first because of the micro under the table and secondly because people seem to be saying much the same thing about the British.'

'The British have had it!' Elissa said with an unexpected harshness in her voice. 'Of course I'm a little prejudiced, you understand, on account of what my husband did or did not do. But I've been seriously thinking of applying for my American citizenship to be restored.'

'And then what?'

'Go to the States of course.'

'A widow with two growing children and no welfare state? You wouldn't last six months.'

'Who says I'm a widow?'

'It might be better if you were.'

'That's a cruel, horrible thing to say.' Then, seeing she had hurt him, she took his hand quietly and went on: 'I'm sorry to go on about Paul, but don't say things like that. You don't know how dangerous they are.' Then, as if she had said too much, she pleaded: 'Don't spoil it, Rupert. I'm enjoying the evening as I haven't for years.'

'I'd like them to go on,' he said; 'the evenings, I mean, and us.'

'I don't suppose Claudia would agree.'

'That's the understatement of the year.' He lit a cigarette. 'Oh, my God! Claudia . . .' he said. 'Don't let's get started on that.'

'But I want to know how it is.'

The fire in his veins was now setting the undergrowth ablaze. Mister Near Miss disappeared once more into the shadows. And stay there, you decrepit old bastard! Rupert said to himself. He ordered more brandies and moved his chair slightly so that their hands might continue to touch.

'You know how it is with Claudia. You saw it in the five minutes you were together in the Embassy. What else is there to say?'

'Why did you never have children?'

A good question that. Because God didn't will it that way – but what if God were putting the question at some celestial Old Bailey? So answer it now.

'To begin with she didn't want any. Then when she did and it was still practicable, the Almighty withheld them.' Yes you did, you old reprobate, he muttered to himself. I did make the attempt . . . well, once or twice.

'You'd have made a good father, I would have thought.'

'Perhaps I still will – don't you think?'

'Speaking generally, yes, Rupert, I think you might.'

'Let's not generalize for too long. I have a time factor too so far as you are concerned.' Instinctively, almost in panic, he gripped her hand and then plunged. The long giddy drop. 'I love you, Elissa, and I want you to marry me!'

She sat absolutely quiet and still, looking at his hand on hers on the chequered tablecloth. The *bouzouki* music went on endlessly from the nearby house. In the distance the lights of Athens twinkled across the bay.

'Oh, Rupert . . .' she said softly in the end and then sighed.

He too fell silent, aware of his almost imperceptible breathing. He did not press her, knowing that anything he then said would be wrong, endlessly prolonging the pause. Then gently she freed her hand from his, giving him a little pressure from the fingers.

'I ought to be getting back,' she said. 'Lucy may be awake and I'd hate her to be frightened by herself in that house. She wouldn't make a sound, just lie there wide-eyed and afraid. She's still a little young for a trip like this.'

He summoned the waiter and paid the bill. By the time they had reached the door of the *taverna* and were exchanging '*Poli kalas*' and '*Efaristo polis*' with the proprietor, the Embassy car had been brought to the door. They were always under surveillance. But for once he did not observe Mister Near Miss in among the watchers in the shadows; nor, when he ran his trained eye over the other cars in the courtyard, did he see anything to arouse suspicion. Major Axley had, in fact, taken good care not to be seen himself, as he kept his own private watch not only on the ambassadorial car but on a Skoda with Corps Diplomatique number plates, which also happened to be there and which followed at a tactful distance.

When they reached the Palazzo Marides there was no one around except for the white-coated, white-gloved servant who let them in. She took him up to see Mark and Lucy, who were both sound asleep in their respective rooms, and then on a sudden impulse she said:

'Come and see the royal boudoir they've given me.'

He followed her into the palatial bedroom with the four-poster bed and the magnificent panoramic view of the moonlit Aegean stretching away below the windows. She insisted that he walked to the balcony 'for a better perspective', and when he turned back she had stripped to her panties and bra, her mouth hungrily seeking for his almost before he could catch his breath. There was a violence and an urgency in her lovemaking as though three years of pent-up passion were almost literally tearing her apart. Deftly she helped him undress and then he took her blindly and with a force he had never experienced before. When his climax came he gave a deep terrible groan which she silenced with her mouth as she stroked his back and told him he mustn't cry. Then they lay in each other's arms in complete and utter peace for an aeon of time.

Outside the villa the driver of the ambassadorial car relieved himself in the bushes and helped himself to a slug of stolen Embassy brandy which he kept for such occasions in a flask by the driver's seat. Farther out on the main road itself the Skoda and Axley, and now for good measure a Greek police car, patiently waited.

'Now you must go,' she murmured at last, 'or there'll be a diplomatic incident. Just get dressed and slip out.'

'I don't think I will,' he said. 'This is the alpha and omega, and beginning and end of it all.'

But she suddenly sat up in a rage. 'Hurry up!' she said, almost spitting the words. 'Anyone can find us here!'

'Anyone?' he said lazily, but the old mechanism of orderly life had started up again and he was only playing for time – time which he knew he couldn't possibly have or use.

'The children!' she said. 'I'd die if they found you here!'

Obediently he retrieved his clothes from their interesting position on the floor and made himself as little dishevelled as possible.

'Hurry, hurry!' she said, beating her fist on the bed. 'And don't make a noise with the door!' He tried to kiss her goodbye but she pushed him angrily away, and a few moments later he was walking quietly along the marble corridor and down the curving staircase to the main room where everything had begun.

Jean-Pierre Mournier rose from a seat by the window.

'You've been seeing the children,' he said with a polite Gallic smile. 'Ils sont bien endormis toute la soirée, I am happy to say. Was the lobster good?'

'Very. Thank you. And now I must go.'

Mournier saw him to the door where the car was waiting outside.

'I hope we shall be seeing you and Mrs Eynsham on Sunday,' he said. 'When I say "we" I am speaking, of course, for the Marides. It should be an interesting day.'

They exchanged a handshake and brief 2 AM smiles, and then the ambassadorial car was speeding away along the dusty, yellowish drive, with Rupert smiling to himself like a satisfied paladin oblivious of the world ahead.

The satisfied smile came smartly off his face on reaching Kyfyssia. The house had been burgled. Each room had been wildly ransacked, and there were clothes and contents of drawers and cupboards strewn everywhere. He had already dismissed the Embassy chauffeur, and the telephone wires had been cut so that he was forced, in the middle of the night, to fetch the police himself, and also to inform the duty officer at the Embassy that he was out of telephone communication. Raw, angry and exhausted, he got into bed at 5 AM.

The next day almost inevitably he had more work and appointments than he could cope with, and it was not until the following day that Janet and the Embassy staff had the house under control and a new maid installed. The Greek police, who as a matter of routine keep the houses of foreign diplomats under special surveillance, appeared in this case to be at a loss. They were reticent and somewhat bored. Axley told Eynsham he was certain they knew who it was, but were not prepared to proceed. In any case, they observed, the Acting Ambassador must have been fully covered by insurance.

This was not good enough for Claudia, who returned on the Saturday to find most of her jewellery gone. She stormed down to the police and opened it all up, braving insult and that kind of Balkan indifference which Greek officialdom seems to have inherited from five hundred years of Turkish control. She failed completely.

'But I'm not leaving it there. I told that fat ugly slug of a Pappadopoulos or whatever his name is that I was taking it higher.'

'What did he say?'

'Examined that long fingernail he affects, shrugged his shoulders and said something in Greek which I didn't understand.'

'I can guess what it was. You won't get anywhere with him.'

'Won't I just? Anyway I'm getting Eudoxia back. You should never have sacked her in the first place – and behind my back.'

'She's a rotten maid.'

'She's better than the one you got – or your precious Miss Mortimer did. Anyway what were you doing out at that time of night? Trying to get off with your secretary?'

'Claudia, how many more times do I have to tell you? Janet and I are not having an affair. Will you get that into your head?'

'Who were you out with then?'

'I was out, that's all.'

They stared at each other across twenty years of hostile misunderstanding. Yet he was still touched to see how unhappy she was. The old helplessness in the face of his personal destiny came flooding back.

'So Eudoxia was right,' Claudia said bitterly. 'You were out with that Tarnham bitch.'

The Greeks knew everything. For Claudia to be told that snippet of information by a maid he had sacked some days before meant only one thing – he was webbed in by a carefully developing plot at the centre of which Elissa was twisting and turning.

'Do you usually discuss my social life with the maid?' he asked, coldly furious.

'She volunteered the information herself.'

'I won't have her back in the house. I don't care how awkward it is.'

'She's back.'

'Then I'm off. I'll move into one of the spare rooms at the Embassy. And you can gossip away here with your maid to your heart's content.'

'Oh, Rupert!' Claudia began to cry. 'Why do you have to do these things to me?'

He stormed out of the house and down to the Embassy. It was Saturday afternoon and in a couple of hours they were due to have drinks with the Everitts. He was thinking of ringing up to make an excuse when Axley appeared at the door.

'Hallo, Stephen, I thought you went sailing on Saturday afternoons.'

'Not this one, sir. I've a little too much on my plate for the moment.'

'What can I do for you then?'

He liked the young man. Claudia might say – and frequently did – that soldiering and diplomacy simply do not mix. But then Claudia found so many people insufferable. Moreover her feminine hackles rose at a man knowing more secrets than she did.

'It's about Mrs Tarnham, sir.' The hesitancy was back in the voice. 'I think there's something you ought to know.'

Eynsham toyed with a paper-knife and studied the young messenger of Fate. If he had a son, he wondered in passing, is this the sort of man he would have turned out to be? Being a soldier these days seemed somehow to be such a dated occupation.

'Is this going to be another piece of your good advice?' he asked.

'Well, not exactly, sir. It's just something you ought to know if you're talking to her at all.'

'All right, fire away.'

'She's been in touch with Paul Tarnham – or rather he with her. She has been for some time. In fact he's in touch with her here.'

So at long last they were trusting him with the truth. He studied the boy's face and then picked up his pipe.

'I see ... well, thank you, Stephen. And what are they cooking up?'

'He wants her and the children to join him in – in Russia.'

'And why do you think I should know this colourful fact?'

'Well, sir, officially of course we don't even know if Paul Tarnham's alive, let alone where he is. I think our people want to keep it that way – at any rate for as long as they can. Of course if she does decide to join her husband, we would be very interested to know ahead of the event.'

'Yes, Stephen, I'm rather interested myself.'

'I ... I thought you might be, sir.' Again that unhappy smile. What jobs they give them to do, Eynsham thought. He reached for the telephone. He had better put things right with Claudia, if he could.

'Are you going to the Marides' tomorrow?' he asked.

'Yes, sir. As a matter of fact your secretary got me invited. Young Marides is making a pass at her.'

'I'm sorry to hear that, Stephen. It gives you a little competition.'

'Yes, sir, it does.'

He asked for a line and dialled his home.

'Then let's wish each other luck, shall we?' He nodded a dismissal to Axley and heard Claudia's peevish voice on the line.

'Sorry,' he said. 'Sorry, sorry, sorry. I'll pick you up in an hour's time for the Everitts'. And of course have Eudoxia back. Perhaps she could make us tea for breakfast in future.'

VI

HE realized, when he put down the phone, that simply saying sorry to Claudia was not going to right the affair. He had reacted automatically to a stimulus. He did this expertly and professionally every day of his life. But this crisis was different in kind. This one was fundamental to the whole of his life.

At least he had an hour to himself. The Embassy was deserted except for the duty staff. He considered calling Axley back and plying him further. But this would be a waste of time. Axley was on the other side, however much the two men might like and respect each other. Eynsham knew he was being watched, though perhaps in a more tactful and hidden way, just as much as Elissa and the people around her. He lit a pipe and took a turn in the garden, a tall, distinguished, equivocal man in a loose string bag of uncertainties.

As he perambulated slowly his thoughts homed on Elissa. Now that he knew her, nothing else really mattered at all. He relived her touch and her feel, even remembering the musk of her body. His skin tingled and he ached with longing. She was now more important to him than anyone else in the world. Now he saw things as they were in sharp primary colours. He had to take her and marry her without further delay or be broken on the wheel.

But what was he to do? How could he force the issue? She had implied that she loved her husband and there were the children who needed their father. She had lied about not being in touch with Paul, but this he found unremarkable. Everyone lied about something. Now that she had given herself to him in one way, would she in the other? Would she now trust him with the truth as she knew it herself? What did truth and loyalty mean if you were Elissa Tarnham, the wife of the celebrated defector?

The late afternoon heat was leaving the garden. He sat down on a bench beside one of the palm trees and looked at the elegant house and its immaculate grounds, the epitome of the aristocratic tradition of diplomacy which seemed today to have almost no connexion whatever with the nuclear world. Where had he always gone wrong? This Embassy, which he enjoyed and respected far more than that little runt Harborough, should have been his. Perhaps a similar one lay in the offing and there would be a letter from Stevens in the Monday bag. They should have given him an embassy long ago. There might equally well be nothing in the Monday mail or in any other mail when it mattered. Unease stirred in the shadowy part of his mind.

Elissa drew back his thoughts, and for a moment or so he pictured her naked body and the pleasures she had given him. There lay the peace and contentment and love which he had sought for so long. Yet scale and comparison nudged their way even into that. A man's capacity to give and receive depended not only on the sum total of his life but also of his awareness of that experience and the value he gave it. You did not waste a good wine on a drowsy man. It occurred to him that the keen catlike quality of Elissa's lovemaking might be at least partially caused by the flagellation of the last three years of her life. Even sleeping cats live in a world of claws. He had no doubt at all that the cat herself rarely if ever lost sight of the fact.

And what was he to do about Claudia? He was honest enough with himself to know that in conceding one or two points to Claudia in the domestic war it was self-interest mainly at work. If he was going to make a break it would be at a time of his own choosing. When Elissa said yes and he had got her safely back to England, then he would or could deal with Claudia and his own affairs. For the moment life had to go on as it was – drinks with the Everitts tonight and the Marides' Sunday party tomorrow. Now that Claudia knew about him and Elissa she could well add a complication or two to that. It would indeed be 'interesting', to use that young Frenchman's word, to see how they would handle their presence tomorrow. It was always possible Claudia would refuse to go. He knocked out his pipe and smiled to himself. Possible but not very likely.

Richard Everitt was a dark, bespectacled, somewhat intellectual New Englander whom Claudia described, though fortunately not in his hearing, as a 'better type of American'. In fact Harvard and US Government service had merely put a gloss of sophistication on to a basically nice but tough-minded man. His wife was small, delicately pretty and Jewish. They had four energetic sons, a Volvo station wagon, three cats and a sailing boat at Piraeus. The family was popular in the Athenian diplomatic world and Rupert looked on Dick Everitt as his best local friend.

'I suppose we shall be subjected to more ostentation about that awful boat of theirs,' Claudia said as they drove into Athens. She entertained a total dislike of Rachel Everitt.

'You can cap it this time with Arthurisms. Or do you want your little expedition hushed up?'

'Rupert, there were three other people in that boat beside Arthur and me.'

'A ménage à cinq. And with Arthur at the helm. I hope someone had a camera.'

'I think that sort of joke is repulsive,' Claudia said, staring fixedly at the traffic.

Good old Arthur, Rupert thought. Perhaps he did make it after all.

At the Everitts' there were the usual crowd who went to such parties, a visiting senator and his puzzled-looking wife, a US general and, what was now an accepted feature of life in the Greek capital, the ministry spy or dictator's lackey. These days a technique had been evolved of inviting to any such gathering a colonels' man who could report back on the guests, their general conversation and anything else of interest he could discover or that was put in his way. He was a cheap form of insurance under the régime as it was at that time.

'Which is the baby-sitter for tonight?' Rupert asked as he arrived.

'Over there by the piano in the dark glasses,' Everitt replied without turning his head. 'Lambakis, Security or Police. I'm not sure which. He's new to me. Halloran got him.' Halloran was the American counterpart to Axley whom Rupert was slightly surprised to see at the party and who was engaging the ministry man in conversation.

'We're well armoured tonight,' Rupert murmured as he made the opening moves in the usual chess game of an Embassy party.

'We just like our guests to be happy,' Everitt said. 'Everitt the Ever-ready.'

It was a spacious apartment in the centre of Athens with everything on a lavish American scale. Claudia automatically dismissed it as vulgar, but Rupert was privately and sometimes openly envious. Washington made things as pleasant and easy as possible for their representatives abroad. Whitehall was Whitehall.

Mr Lambakis did not wait to be introduced. He came over and presented himself in excellent English. He gave himself no rank but simply said he was from the Ministry of the Interior. The dark glasses seemed to give him some sort of added and sinister status, like a Greek Tonton Macoute.

'I'm sorry to hear you had burglars the other night.'

'Well, it's the mess and the fuss they cause which is so tedious,' Rupert replied as they sized each other up. It would be a mistake to compliment him on his English. This was no village boy making good in the great capital city. This one had been to Oxbridge without a doubt.

'I'm pretty sure we'll get the jewellery back for Mrs Eynsham. It was a put-up job.'

'Do you know who did it?'

Lambakis gave him a condescending smile. 'Of course,' he said with the full irony in the voice. 'Don't you realize we always know everything these days? From the departure of a king to the theft of a basket of eggs. I'm joking, of course.' Like hell you are, thought Eynsham and smiled in response.

'However,' Lambakis went on, 'I doubt there will be any arrests. When I say we know who did it, I mean – naturally – that we know who caused it to be done. We will secure the return of the jewellery and I am sure full recompense will be made. We Greeks are generous, you know. We are no longer the struggling threadbare nation that I think your colleague Mr Tarnham knew when he was here as a third secretary some years ago. Things have changed a great deal since then.'

Rupert supposed this to be a piece of bait which he did not even bother to nibble. Or was Lambakis simply signalling that everything about him was known? If so he ignored that signal too.

'Who did do it?'

'Oh, the family of your ex-maid who, I understand, you are taking back. It's a fairly familiar pattern. We Greeks are perhaps over-sensitive in our pride. We hate being sacked in a fit of pique. I think Mrs Eynsham is very wise to be taking her back. That way you can be sure of her loyalty and also that it will never happen again. But I'm so sorry you had all that fuss and trouble after such an exhausting evening. We shall try and make amends.'

He glinted a smile through his dark glasses and moved on to talk to the visiting general. Rupert felt he had been dismissed. He must find out from Axley who the gentleman was. Things were astir in Athens.

As soon as he could unnoticeably get away, Axley left the party and picked up Janet at the flat which she shared with three other girls from the Embassy.

'You look stunning,' he said in a somewhat offhand way he had not intended.

'Thank you, Stephen, I love your up-to-the-minute words. You're dead spiffing yourself.'

'Oh, I'm not as bad as all that.' He hated a woman putting him on the defensive. 'All right, groovy or trendy or grotty or whatever you are, let's go and have something to eat.'

'As a matter of fact, it's Axley the preoccupied, isn't it?' Janet said as they drove out to their favourite *taverna*. 'Man of Security!'

He tried to disengage his thoughts from Lambakis, Eynsham, Mrs Tarnham and the Greeks. He had a pretty girl beside him with whom he was falling in love. It was a fine Saturday evening in May. The soft Athenian light, that special clarity which made Greece unique, had never provided him with a more romantic setting. Instead he was entangled in his work like a swimmer among reeds.

'To hell with them all,' he said through his teeth; 'they're even trying to wreck the few moments I have with you.'

'Don't be so serious about it. Let them all spy each other into the ground.'

Then seeing that she could not jeer him out of his mood, she made a play of taking him at his face value. 'All right. What are the developments I can be trusted with? What happened at the Everitts'?'

'There's a new Greek – a colonels' toady – called Lambakis who seems remarkably well informed. He knew the Eynshams' robbery was a put-up job. He made a passing reference to the Tarnham connexion, which might mean anything or nothing. He certainly seems to know who does what in the US and British embassies. He chatted up Halloran about Greek-American Communists, he asked me if I'd met Mrs Tarnham. Of course he may be implying more than he actually knows in the familiar way of the Greeks. But on the other hand he may know more than any of us on why Greece has been chosen for the Tarnham round.'

'What do you mean by that?'

'Surely you see what they're really after, don't you?'

'No – what?'

'Eynsham of course.'

They both fell silent at this. Janet visualized her boss with his tired smiling eyes and that ghastly wife. She could not see a way through the problem and at the moment had no wish to try.

She had no doubt about Eynsham's loyalty herself. Maybe he had his back to the wall for reasons inaccessible to her. She really did not want to know. He was still, in her eyes, a marvellously warm and understanding man. She was on his side.

'You know I feel as you do about the Counsellor,' Axley said eventually as they settled themselves in the *taverna*.

She looked at his solemn face. He was an attractive man, but he seemed to want to cocoon her in a mock seriousness.

She decided to play it his way. 'All right, Stephen, I know. But you have facts and knowledge not available to me. Very well, then, let's forget the whole thing for an hour or two. We're all going to be deep in it tomorrow. By the way, Christos Marides is picking me up after breakfast so I don't need transport.'

She thought this would make him jealous but he was still lost in his thoughts.

'I wonder if there's a young Lambakis like there is a young Marides,' Axley said thoughtfully. 'I rather doubt it.'

'You really are an obsessional man, aren't you? Don't you ever pay attention to the girl you're with?'

He was genuinely sorry and then tried to put it right. He asked her questions about the tennis that afternoon, about the other girls in the apartment, fishing around in a hopelessly inept way for some connexion with the carefree Saturday evening mood he had so looked forward to reaching. He could not shake off the incubus of the job.

'It's like being out with a meter reader,' she said in the end. 'No wonder your wife shoved off back to England. I feel as if you're peering at a lot of dreary dials, taking down jolly little figures, all utterly meaningless to me. I'd have had more fun with Christos Marides. At least I'd be feeling like a girl instead of an animated dictating machine.'

She could almost see him putting himself into another gear.

'Janet – you know I think you're the most attractive thing to hit the British Embassy in years.'

She looked at him incredulously and then laughed. 'You sound like a Press hand-out, Stephen. Honestly, you must cut away from it sometimes. Or at least take it more lightly.'

'Don't you take anything seriously yourself?'

She smiled with her eyes. 'Yes – people. That's why I bother with you.'

At last she got a rise.

'I thought it was the other way round,' he said stiffly. 'It's usual for the man to bother about the woman.'

'Then bother a bit more and get me another drink.'

He did as he was told and thought how nice it would be to go back to active soldiering. As if reading his thoughts she said:

'I don't think you understand women and I don't think you need them except for one specialized purpose. That's how you think about us, isn't it? We're just there for the bed and to do as we're told. Well, there are cheaper ways of buying what you want than this or me.' Then seeing that she had really hurt him, she took his hand. 'Sorry, Stephen. I didn't mean that. You're all right – underneath.'

That night as Eynsham lay in bed, listening to Claudia's quiet breathing, he felt a chill of loneliness such as he had not experienced since adolescence. There was no one to whom he could turn. Claudia was locked away in her prejudice, and in any event he wished their relationship to end. In the Embassy he had no contemporaries to whom he could let off steam or, even in ordinary discussion, find out if the miseries which dogged him day and night had any real base. Accidentally or by intent he was isolated.

Who was Lambakis and how did he know so much? Why had young Axley decided to warn him about Tarnham almost accidentally and late on Saturday afternoon? Why was Elissa so deeply evasive? The trap was certainly set. But now there was a further and troubling conclusion to draw. Perhaps they were hoping to have business with him.

'Can't you get to sleep?' Claudia asked irritably. 'Why don't you take a pill?'

He looked across at her beaky face in the shadows.

He had meant to pick his moment and do it according to plan but now it came tumbling out.

'I'll tell you why I can't get to sleep. It's because of you. You – Claudia. I think it's time we packed it up, you and I. I can't stand it any more.'

'You always say that,' she taunted, 'and then you do nothing about it.'

'How can I? Here in Athens? I can't just walk out of the Embassy. You'll have to cooperate. I'll give you a divorce.'

'Thank you. I don't want a divorce. Anyway you don't think that Tarnham bitch is going to take you on, do you? Or are you still in cloud cuckoo land?'

'I thought I was supposed to be having it off with my secretary?'

He always regretted a descent into sarcasm, but every time this seemed the only weapon she left him.

'Well, Rupert, as I've told you before, if you want a divorce you'll have to do something about it yourself. You can't expect me to cut my own throat – nor will any judge either. You're wasting your time. I've no intention of budging.'

'I'll cite Arthur.'

'I wish you would. He'd strip you of what little money you have. At least he's not a complete fool in the ways of the world.'

'We can't go on like this. We'll end up strangling each other.'

He felt very like doing it then.

'Talk, talk, talk. That's your life all over. Talk and no action.'

'There's going to be some action now!' he said grimly, knowing as he said it that this was no more than a shout in the dark. A shout of despair. They had him hemmed in on all sides. But suppose Elissa said yes? Suppose by some miracle Claudia agreed to release him, Elissa got her own divorce and once back in England they were free to be married? Another chill struck him. He would have to retire or resign from the Service. They would never allow him to marry Paul Tarnham's wife after all that had happened and then entrust him with an embassy of his own. The taint remained. Il m'a vraiment emmerdé, ce couillon-là, he thought and wondered, as he had done a thousand times over the last three years, why of all people it had to happen to him. Why? But there was never an answer to this, least of all in the dark watches of the night.

VII

WHATEVER the realities behind the Greek dictatorship, it was evident to Elissa that money still talked in Athens. She had no idea how political a person Panayotis Marides had been or was at this time. But he certainly used his great wealth to buy privilege. The house ran with the smoothness of an international luxury hotel. People came and went, dinners and parties seemed to be given without any apparent regard to the political restrictions she knew to be in force. Early in her stay she had asked her host about this.

'Restrictions? Restrictions are for other people.'

'You talk like le Roi Soleil.'

'He had the right idea, that Louis.' Although he spoke perfect English Marides could drop into Greek-American idiom at the flick of an eyelid, 'So why you worry your head? I fix you things here. I fix the world.'

'I think maybe you do.'

'Not so much of the maybe. You want I should buy you something? Like a yacht, a house, a country, a king? All things are possible.'

'Not a Greek king surely?'

'Ay-ay-ay. A Greek king is a little difficult. Needsa some thought. But why you ask silly questions like that? Relax. Enjoy yourself. Feel yourself at home.'

'I thought people weren't supposed to have large private parties in their houses?'

'Ach!' Marides made a particular Eastern Mediterranean noise of contempt with that Greek flick of the fingers from under the chin which conveys a visual derisive no. 'Who was it said, "Justice, like the Ritz bar, is open to all"?'

'I don't think he was Greek.'

'He is now. Stop worrying, Elissa – enjoy yourself for a while in the sun. You are under powerful protection.'

She gave him a hard look. 'Yes, I'm aware of that.'

At another time he had reminded her that all dictators need to have international fixers available and cooperative. If Hong Kong had not happened to be there, the Chinese Communists would have had to invent it. Like Switzerland for the Nazis. But she was not basically interested in money, as he was, so he did not develop the idea.

'Why are you really doing all this for us?' she had asked, but as always he had evaded a direct reply.

'Don't ask silly questions like that when you know most of the answers.'

'But I don't.'

'Well, one or two of them then. Is there something you want – that you don't have here?'

She had been equally quick at deflecting the conversation. 'The children are lonely. Children need other children to play with.'

It was as if she had been ordering materials for a party at Harrods. The next day some ten children had been delivered to the beach. They had been of mixed nationalities, but all were from families like the Marides with international and diplomatic connexions. They had actually made things worse for Mark and Lucy, who were driven into their shells. Only Jean-Pierre Mournier seemed to understand. He acted as a catalyst, and by the Sunday of the archaeological picnic had become the children's trusted friend.

Marides' ex-wife Helen arrived from Paris on the Saturday evening. She was in almost every respect the opposite of Panayotis. She had been of much better upbringing, but was also endowed with the inhibitions and ladylike neuroses behind which her Edwardian parents had hedged in their lives at the beginning of the century. Where Panayotis was ebullient, she was nervous and highly strung. As the Marides fortunes continued to prosper, she had perforce had to come to terms with the commercial world in which her husband operated. She had not enjoyed it. Elissa had got to know her slightly when she and Paul had done their first tour of duty in Athens. She had always struck Elissa as a minor character in a Chekov play, one of the sisters who would never make Moscow, but the non-Chekovian factor was the Marides wealth. This had progressively drained away any pathos in the relationship between the pushing Greek-Cypriot boy and the threadbare near-aristocratic girl he had married. Money had been the solvent. Once Christos had been conceived, she had been able to deny Panayotis the messy sexual rights he had earlier on demanded. Whereas her own mother had had the vapours, Helen had taken up with art and archaeology, and Panayotis had indulged his fancies elsewhere in line with his international life. They were oil and water and soon neither made any attempt to mix. Now divorce, alimony and an elegant Paris life amongst the sexually neutered had allowed her to enjoy the style and the pattern of the life she had wanted as a child without having to put up with Panayotis either in her bed or in the unpredictable, explosive moments he imposed on their social life. If Panayotis was le Roi Soleil, she was the exiled queen with her psychiatry, religion and the dainty sterility with which she scented her life.

But Panayotis found her useful from time to time. There was also a certain residue of affection expressed in mutual insult which both enjoyed. She knew there was purpose in everything he did and it no longer upset her. In return the *émigré* epicene friends who floated in and out of her life made Panayotis laugh and he enjoyed patronizing them at one remove.

'Why was it so important for me to come this weekend?' she asked him when they were alone.

'Business.'

She gave him a withering look. 'Was there ever anything else?'

'You get on with Mrs Eynsham, don't you?'

'Not especially. She has a taste for archaeology. I'm rather sorry for her.'

'Develop it this weekend. Keep her away from her husband.'

'And Elissa Tarnham?'

'Leave that side of things to me.'

'What are you up to now?'

'You know I never answer that sort of question. What archaeological debauch did you have in mind for tomorrow?'

'I've asked Professor Grenier-Laborde for the day. I thought we might have a look at the Temple of Poseidon. He talks rather well.'

'Keep him at it as long as you can.'

'Is it true you have a big deal with the Russians?'

He was able to return her withering look. 'What Russians?' he said. 'What deal?'

When they woke up in the morning the children had got into the habit of climbing into their mother's bed and discussing the day ahead. They were still not really at ease in all the luxury which surrounded them. The shabby old flat in Fulham was a million miles away, but it was still their home. However, she had managed to get them to go wandering down to the beach when they were tired of snuggling in bed. She could keep an eye on them from the balcony of her room, and she could pamper herself with breakfast in bed and an endlessly slow bath to start off the day. For Elissa it was time out from the mother-and-father act and the getting-them-off-to-school with which her London days began.

But they were not really happy. They missed their friends. The luxury of the house, even the beach and the expeditions were only a partial compensation for the company of other children. How then would it be if she took them to Russia, as Paul was demanding? She supposed they would have a nasty six months or a year and then they would grow up as Russian children. But at least they would have a father. Up to now she had not been able to tell them even that he was alive. Children tell other children, they had warned her, and no one was to know or the letters would stop. Even those she had occasionally received had had to be burnt as soon as she had read them. And now, as a further complication, there was Rupert. The children wriggled and squabbled beside her in bed while she wondered what sort of father Rupert would make if she were to say yes to him. As if there was a telepathic connexion between them, Mark suddenly said:

'When is Father coming to see us, Mummy?'

She lay with her eyes closed for a moment or so to give herself time. 'We don't know officially if he's still alive.'

'Jean-Pierre says he is.'

So that was the link. She felt the adrenalin pumping into her system and fought back the rage which threatened to swamp her. How dare they impose this three years' silence on her and then let someone like Jean-Pierre Mournier break it to her children? For a few seconds she was so angry she could not speak. Then she regained the familiar icy control.

'How does he know, Mark? And what has he told you?'

'Just that Daddy's somewhere in Russia and we might be seeing him again.'

'Do you want to go to Russia, if that's where he is?' She hated herself and she hated them – the 'them' of both sides – for the deceptive routine which enveloped her life and her relationships even with her own children. She knew where Paul was, so what else except habit had made her say 'if that's where he is'? The trouble was that once indoctrinated in the security mould of thought, the fear of blackmail, the fear that something would happen to Paul because of a slip on her part, had entered her marrow and now affected her daily life down to the smallest detail. But she was going to talk basically to Jean-Pierre. How dare they do this to her? She toyed with the thought of packing up there and then and of going on the next aircraft to London.

'Oh yes,' said Mark, 'let's go to Russia!'

'No,' Lucy said, snuggling in close to her mother; 'let's go home.'

'If we went to Russia that would have to be our home,' she said. Now it was out to the children, they would all be in a different position. It was no good telling them to keep their mouths shut about their father's whereabouts. Soon it would be common knowledge that the celebrated Paul Tarnham was where he had long been suspected: in Russia – just another expatriate of diminishing political value who had opted out, leaving behind him the wreckage of a family life. For the millionth time she said bitterly to herself: 'How could you do this to me – to your children – to us?'

'Time you went down to the beach,' she said brusquely and got them moving. When she was alone the anger returned so that she found herself actually beating the bed with her fists. Yet of course it could never be so simple as it first appeared. Paul himself was a deep and complicated man. And where was Marides in it all? What was she doing out here in these rich, unaccustomed surroundings? Why had Mournier let the cat out of the bag to her children and not first of all to her? She had lived with the problem long enough to know that there was no such thing as an accidental move in the life she had been forced to lead. She got up determined to have it out with young Monsieur Mournier as soon as she could get hold of him.

But Mournier was nowhere to be found that morning, and once Elissa had gone down on the beach the immediacy of her anger melted away. At any time *chez* Marides there were usually some half-dozen house guests around of all sorts and sizes. It was like a club, and this morning a young German shipping man and his Siamese wife took her water-skiing before the Sunday lunchtime crowd arrived. There were always distractions. She had become in her own eyes an expert in detachment, but the interaction of her outer and her inner life continued to keep her in lively suspense. The woman who lay in bed raging at the unfairness of all that had happened was not the same woman who for the first time in her life tried and succeeded in skiing on one ski with the exhilaration this produced. The martini-drinking Joan Mathews on the Marides' private beach seemed to her own eyes to be different in kind from the harassed London mother in her Victorian apartment. Then again, the wife whose husband had left her without warning for deep-seated ideological reasons she could scarcely take in was somehow of different texture from the woman whose lover was coming to lunch and who would sooner or later be forced to a decision about the next phase of her life.

She left the speedboat and went up to the house to change. Physically she felt ten years younger than when she had arrived in Greece. The sun and the sea had restored the lithe, tawny qualities of her body. She had always been the cat who walked alone, and now the holiday had given back to her the feline pleasure in her body she had had as a girl. As she showered and examined her figure critically in the many-mirrored bathroom she pushed away in her mind the murky insecurity of the last three years and the problems she knew lay almost immediately ahead. She did not see herself doing this in Russia, but then she knew nothing but hearsay of the life Paul had decided to adopt. Perhaps there were luxurious dachas on the Black Sea where auburn cats could preen themselves in sexily placed mirrors. She somehow doubted it, but the child in her stubbornly refused to give up hope. She felt almost breathlessly alive, and for that alone she was grateful.

The Ambassador had been expected to return that Sunday evening, but there was a telegram when Rupert looked in at the Embassy after breakfast saying that he would be further delayed.

'Now I really can praise the Lord with joyful heart,' Rupert remarked as he and Claudia set off for church.

'If you took the trouble to get on better terms with the Harboroughs—' Claudia began.

'I'd still be exactly where I am,' he cut in. 'I resigned from the arse-lickers' club a long time ago.'

'I wish you wouldn't use those disgusting expressions!'

'Well, it's Sunday. One has to do something for the Lord.'

His sleepless night had left him raw and red-eyed, his anxieties fermenting inside him as if he were hung over. He was able to pin-point the reason for this as they walked into the church. He was almost physically afraid of meeting Elissa again. He felt as jittery as a schoolboy before a sports day event.

'You look very calm and collected,' Claudia remarked, 'considering the vile things you said to me last night.'

'Just get on with the praying,' he whispered; 'it might do both of us good.'

He knew she could not stand his frivolity, but Oh dear God, how else could he get through the day beset as he was? Steady now, Eynsham, he told himself as the sparse congregation began the first valiant hymn, bluff is supposed to be your *métier* even in the house of God. And God only knows what you really are and how the celestial cookie is going to crumble. That is if it was going to crumble at all. The possibility that it might not struck him with paralysing force. Maybe limbo was for ever.

During the service his state of nerves got worse instead of better, so that at one moment he thought he might be having a heart attack. But this passed, and as it did so he suddenly remembered where he had met Lambakis before. The heavy Levantine face – was he really Greek? – that sensual mouth and the habit of wearing dark glasses even at night, the ability to convey a threat even in the way he moved – these were all part of the stock-in-trade, as he had then phrased it, of the head of a somewhat questionable oil company operating out of Macao or Hong Kong – or was it the Argentine? That was more likely, and he had had to do with the dictator – Peron. It was all coming back to him. Lambakis had been a 'self-exported Greek', and someone had remarked on his being a man to watch. Ironically the boot was now on the other foot. Poor Greece, he thought with an unexpected twinge of pity, all the international operators were moving in under cover of the dictatorship as they had done in every similar country in the world, working in secrecy, relying on force and doing unknown favours for unknown financial rewards.

As the service went on his thoughts played about the Marides family, whose hospitality he would soon be accepting. Of course Panayotis Marides was a bigger international fish than Lambakis. He would survive if Greece itself ceased to exist. It was therefore more likely to be to the benefit of the régime to keep in with Marides rather than the other way round. But where did the Tarnhams come into this? He could not see where the significance lay and perhaps, conceivably, there was no significance in it at all. Nevertheless as the tired little service came to an end and the surviving governesses with their reticules tottered away in the sunlight, Rupert felt his instincts signalling danger as if some part of his being was already aware of what lay immediately ahead.

VIII

THE feeling of being a guest at the court of a medieval princeling, miraculously transplanted into the twentieth century, was particularly noticeable on Sundays whenever Panayotis Marides happened to be in residence in Greece. Everything was on a caviare scale. An acid columnist had once dismissed 'this Greek exhibitionism' as a mixture of the worst of eighteenth-century England and of Hollywood in the twenties and thirties. But the blend was more subtle than that. Moreover it was simply a pattern repeated, though under different climatic conditions, at the Marides establishments at Sunningdale, Westchester and Cap Martin.

Indeed, except for the lavish quantities of food and drink

and the staff to ferry it around, there was nothing especially vulgar in the parties Marides gave. He was possessed of a large and luxurious house in a particularly beautiful part of the Greek coastline, and the considerable estate also contained sufficient antiquities to interest those who were archaeologically minded. Between speedboats and ruins there was something for everyone's taste.

Panayotis had acquired the land and built his great house partly as an act of defiance. The son of a peasant whose *stremma* were divided up into twenty-five different places, he had known since a boy how difficult it was to put together a large estate in Greece. Here was a country where the laws of primogeniture are virtually unknown and where death will forcibly divide a farm into equal parts among the descendants. But Greece was still his native country and he knew how his countrymen thought. Patiently and forcefully and at a very considerable cost he had step by step bought the land he required, using money he had made elsewhere in the world, an importation which endeared him to the Greek authorities.

'My father's pride in achieving all this', Christos explained to Janet as he showed her round, 'is only exceeded by my own complacent knowledge that one day it will all be mine.' He gave her a glistening smile. 'And of course I'm sure you already know Greece well enough', he went on, 'never to believe anything you're told by a Greek such as myself. We simply can't be relied on at all.'

He was a good-looking young man, Janet thought, as the *Thunderbird* was put through its paces for her benefit, but inordinately fond of himself. Or was that another consciously fostered deception? As if he were reading her thoughts he shot her a glance and asked:

'On what you know of us so far, do you find the Greeks easy to understand?'

'Oh yes,' she answered cheerfully, 'I can read you all like a book. In Chinese.'

Altogether some forty to fifty guests had been asked to lunch, of whom about a dozen had been earmarked by

Helen Marides for her professor's audience at the Temple of Poseidon in the afternoon. The rest were allowed to swim, water-ski or do what they pleased. Two members of the ruling clique were present, with their wives, which made the party A1 at Lloyd's.

By the time the Eynshams arrived the pre-lunch drinking on the terrace was well under way. While he and Claudia were welcomed by their host and hostess with the deference still appropriate to the Ambassador of Great Britain, his practised eye picked out the German and Dutch ambassadors, the Liberian representative and a couple of sinister Chinese in the prison uniforms they affected these days. He shook hands with Helen Marides and took it all in without appearing to have looked round the room. As he downed his first martini and asked what the weather was like in Paris, he spotted Elissa in the corner talking to the wife of another Greek shipowner whom they knew and there were three or four heavily built Slavs looking like disaffected extras in a bad spy film. Janet, Christos Marides, Axley and the young French diplomat who was a house guest were talking down below on the next step of the terrace, and Rupert noted with amusement the stiff resentment exuding from Axley towards Marides, who had his arm round Janet's waist illustrating some skiing technique.

It took a little time to separate himself from Claudia, and except for one short concentrated look he and Elissa showed no signs of recognition. Usually at these parties Claudia was only too eager to sail away on her own out of her husband's inhibiting presence, but today she seemed to cling almost instinctively to his nearness. Helen Marides introduced her to Professor Grenier-Laborde and they discovered they had mutual university friends. The professor at once began discussing the book on Cretan mythology which he was writing, and Claudia in turn tried to engage his interest in a manual she planned on Mediterranean gardening, a subject the professor quite clearly thought to be of staggering boredom.

Thus lunch came and went. The Temple of Poseidon was

at Sounion, a half-hour away, and there were, so the professor maintained, some newly discovered caves nearby to which he had secured access and which it would be rewarding to visit. But Claudia was refusing the bait.

'I don't feel up to it,' she said in Rupert's ear; 'it's too hot and I'm not well.'

'You could have a snooze in the car.'

'You just want to get rid of me.'

'Nonsense. You're the one who's interested in archaeology. Curl up with a good ruin and have yourself a gay afternoon.'

'You're impossible!'

'Well, what *do* you want to do? You're one of the principal people the Marides have gone to all this trouble to entertain. Am I to take you home instead?'

'You're only trying to get into bed with that Tarnham bitch.'

'Claudia, there are roughly fifty people at this party. How do you think I'm going to achieve it? Pull yourself together, for God's sake!'

'Oh, Rupert, I had a terrible dream last night,' Claudia said, and looked so unhappy that in spite of his irritation Rupert felt suddenly stricken. 'I feel something awful is going to happen.'

'Now then you two' – Helen Marides bustled daintily into this whispered exchange – 'I've come to split up husband and wife. I thought we'd leave in about ten minutes,' she went on to Claudia, without giving her time to answer; 'the Gräfin is coming too and one of those silent Chinese, though what he's going to get out of it I cannot imagine, as they don't appear to speak English, Greek, French or any intelligible language. Of course I suppose it's *vieux jeu* to talk about the mysterious East, but I sometimes think our parents were right. Anyway Pan tells me he's doing some sort of deal about aircraft spares with the other one and so he wants ours – the crinkly one with the big ears – out of the way for a couple of hours. I know I can count on your help, can't I, my dear?'

'I was thinking that perhaps you wanted me out of the way as well,' Claudia blurted out, looking across the room at Elissa. Helen Marides pretended to misunderstand.

'My dear Claudia, I can't imagine what's in your mind,' she said with the sort of trill her governesses used to give all those centuries ago. 'I've come on purpose from Paris just to give the professor an appreciative audience and I'm relying on you to help. After all he is one of the most distinguished experts in the world. We can't leave him talking away to himself now, can we?'

'Why don't you come too, Rupert?' Claudia asked. A sick twinge arrowed his guts. His wife's twisted, beaky face reminded him of a swimmer reaching out for a lifeline. He looked quickly away in dismay. She would do anything to ram the guilt down squarely on his shoulders.

'Oh, God,' he said, 'you know how I am about ruins! I feel more like a swim, anyway.' He was determined to keep it light. 'I'd probably pose the worthy professor some sensationally stupid question and find we were shut out of the Common Market all over again. You know how it is with French intellectuals and square old Anglo-Saxon diplomats.' He shot another glance at her troubled face. It was hopeless. He decided to give in. 'All right, Claudia, I'll come along if you really want it that way.'

She sighed and looked as if she was going to cry. 'It doesn't matter. It was silly of me to ask.'

Helen Marides, whose social timing was diplomatically geared, quickly took her by the arm and urged her away.

'I do think we might let the men have what they want. After all, it is Sunday afternoon.'

He watched Claudia being led away as if she were an ox in an *abattoir*. She did not look back, nor did she glance at Elissa across the room. But she had achieved what, consciously or unconsciously, she had set out to do. She left him crotchety with guilt and it was with relief that he found Janet and Axley at his side urging him to come down to the beach for a swim. The party was breaking up into its component sections and Rupert had already observed

Panayotis and the other Chinese disappearing together. He fetched his bathing things from the car and followed them down to the beach.

The cool Aegean changed his mood and took care of the lunchtime martinis. After his swim he joined Elissa and the children, who were with Jean-Pierre Mournier. He was anxious to make a good impression on the children, but they were disarmingly antagonistic. Mark shook hands politely and then mooched off to his aquarium: Lucy actually shrank away by her mother's side and it took some minutes of desultory conversation before Mournier could persuade her to go exploring with him. This left Janet and Axley, who themselves showed every intention of sticking around until Eynsham was forced into saying: 'Stephen, be a good chap and shove off, will you? I want a few private words with Mrs Tarnham.'

'Of course.' Axley dragged Janet away, trying to make a joke of his discomfiture and failing completely in the process.

'God! The way one has to spell everything out these days,' Rupert said as he settled down beside her on the beach. 'We don't seem to have much time, do we?'

'I was wondering how and when you'd arrange it.'

'It was all I could do to get Claudia off to her stone remains. She seems to know about us, by the way.'

'What about us?'

'The other night. I told you we'd been burgled when I got back. Well, the maid I sacked seems to run a private detective and gossip agency. She told Claudia you and I had been dining together that night. I don't know what else she knows.'

'There isn't very much else, is there?'

'Is that how you view it today?'

'View what? I don't think there is a view.'

'No?'

'Oh, Rupert,' she said, relenting a little, 'I don't know what to do!'

'Marry me.'

'If it were just as easy as that. But you know it isn't, for either of us. And what would happen to your career if I did?'

'Nothing much seems to be happening to my career as things are.'

'I wouldn't exactly be of help though, would I?'

'It's a risk I'm ready to take.'

'I don't think the Foreign Office would. You and Paul Tarnham's wife propping up some sensitive post on the Communist perimeter – and if you retired from the Service, what would you do – for money I mean?'

'Do you love me, Elissa?'

She drew little pictures in the sand with her finger. 'I don't know, Rupert. I think possibly I do. Do you love me?'

'Yes, Elissa, as well you know.'

There was another long pause.

'I've heard from Paul,' she eventually said, still looking at the sand. 'He wants us to join him.' So at last she had decided to trust him. His heart leapt and he smiled like a boy.

'I'm glad you finally told me.'

'You knew all along?'

'Oh, come along now, darling – no catechisms. Apart from anything else, there isn't time.'

'*Did* you know all along?'

She was looking at him now and he returned her a steady gaze. A shiver of wariness hit him in the spine. Why was it so important to her to know? After all she was the one concerned. He turned the question back on her. Somewhere on his Foreign Office confidential file was a note saying that he could be a tough negotiator, but only when interested enough.

'Well, if it comes to that, did *you*?'

'Not before it happened. Of course not. He just went. But shortly afterwards when he fetched up where he intended. Then I knew. Of course.'

'And you never told our people? Never once?'

'I couldn't even let on to the children. That was the hardest of all.'

'Bloody blackmail!' Rupert said through his teeth. 'Why? What did they want from you?'

'He was my *husband*, Rupert – don't you understand? Those were his *children*. Instincts are very primitive when you get down to levels like that. I'd had enough attention from the Press for ten lifetimes. And that goes for the grilling and interrogation as well.'

'You became an expert liar.' He wanted to ask why she had lied to him, but he sheered away from putting this particular question.

'I lie all the time. It's second nature now.'

During the pause which followed two of the other guests passed by and asked Rupert some question about Windsor Castle.

'British embassies have become nothing but glorified travel agencies!' Rupert remarked sharply when they had gone. 'We're all going to end up as tourists in one another's countries.' But he was thinking of other things. He wanted time: time to try to work out the implications of what she had just been saying. The confrontation mood was in danger of evaporating away into nothing, but he was also aware of an urgency tingling in his blood.

'We've so little time,' he went on, 'I can't think why you didn't trust me before.'

'You so easily get into the habit of trusting no one at all.'

'Not even me.'

She looked at him with the deep smoky question in her eyes. 'No, I think you're different. At least I hope you are.'

'Why did you come out to Greece?'

'You know the answer to that. To get away from it all. To try and make up my mind.'

'Are you a Communist? Or I believe it's more fashionable these days to say Marxist.'

'You know I'm not.'

'I really know nothing about that side of you at all.'

'I'm not a political person.'

'You were.'

This touched one of the well-springs of anger which lay so near the surface in her being.

'When I was a girl – of course. At the university – who isn't? I mean, what's the point of going to university unless you do hammer that side of things out for yourself? But that's a long time ago. I've grown up since then – married Paul – had children – had something of a life.'

'Why didn't you go with Paul?'

'He went on impulse. That was the sort of person he was. I didn't know he was going. He didn't take me into his confidence.' She looked out into the distance. 'And I was his wife.' She was staggeringly attractive to him. The sculptured face, the grey-green eyes and the lean rangy body drew him irresistibly to touch her, to want to possess her there and then, to envelop her with his arms and never let her go. The animal chemistry between them was very potent. He wondered if she felt anything of the same intensity of magnetism as he did at that moment.

'But since then?' he persisted. 'Surely he's been urging you to join him for three long years?'

'It isn't as simple as that. You'd know if you were me. I have a life as well – and the children come into it.'

'Or is it me? Had something already started up between us before he went? You know it had for me.'

She laughed. 'You're asking the questions and answering them all in one breath. You're very boyish when you're like that – for all the grey hairs on your head.' She touched his hand. 'I'm very fond of you, Rupert. You surely know that?'

'You're so good at dodging, my sweet. Was it because of me that you came to Greece?'

'A little bit perhaps.'

It was all he could do to go on. He wanted her so much he had almost to give himself a physical push to ask the one question which could not be avoided. He watched Christos Marides water-skiing with Janet, and in passing smiled ironically at what he knew Axley's reaction would be. He gave her a quick glance and put the knife in.

'But surely you came out here under orders to meet me. Isn't that so?'

'Orders from whom?'

'From Paul's new friends – or old ones for all I know.' There was a long pause. Her fingers still played about in the sand. 'Well, isn't that so?'

'I don't take orders, Rupert.'

'Anyone takes orders when there are favours the other end – for husbands, wives and children.'

'I said I'd meet you and see how you were – that's all.'

'Well, thank you for being honest about that.' The emotion was now changing to anger.

'How did you know?'

'I didn't. I guessed.'

'They're interested in you. That's all I know. I don't know why. I don't want to know.'

'I dare say,' he said with some asperity; 'however, I'd like to know myself. Oddly enough.'

'They said you were "half sour" – I think that was the expression they used.'

'Did they now?' By this time he was really angry.

She turned to him quickly. 'Rupert, I had no idea we were going to fall in love. That wasn't in the calculation at all. It changes it basically for me.'

'But you were aware of how I'd begun to feel three years ago. You knew I was on the hook.'

'An infatuation is one thing. Fishing deliberately for people is another.'

'Don't kid yourself, darling, you're fishing all right – and in somewhat troubled waters, if I may coin a phrase.'

She looked him steadily in the eyes. 'You're wrong about that. I'm doing nobody's dirty work. I've enough trouble trying to plan things out for myself.'

'Then what are you supposed to do?'

'Just tell them how you are.'

'And how am I?'

'So far as I can see, completely unchanged. Just as you were three years ago.'

'Oh no I'm not!' he said bitterly. 'Three years ago I still had some hope. All right – what's the next move?'

'The next move is a swim,' she said, getting up and walking down quickly to the sea.

IX

IT HAD not been much of an afternoon for Stephen Axley. He had no natural taste for this extravagant hospitality. He would have preferred to go sailing. Then in addition his feelings were raw from the blunder he had made with the Counsellor, in sticking around so long and so obviously that Eynsham had had to ask to be left with Madame. Finally that oily young Greek had swept Janet away from under his nose. Altogether the day was a drag.

He silently cursed the Tarnham woman, hard as a chisel and probably being put to much the same use; he cursed Eynsham for allowing himself to become once more involved; he cursed his wife Fiona for marrying him and then messing him up; and finally he cursed himself for being fool enough to take up a job for which he knew himself to be basically unsuited. In this confused state of mind he wandered along the beach to the place where the Tarnham children had their aquarium in a dammed-up rock pool, and where the young Frenchman was playing with them.

'Hallo, Mark. Hallo, Lucy.'

'Hallo.'

They both looked at him with a suspicion he found disconcerting, as if he were intending to do them a violence.

Mournier smiled. 'They're still rather shy, Major Axley.'

'They don't seem to be with you. I don't think we've met, have we?'

'Jean-Pierre Mournier. I'm a house guest at the Marides'.'

They shook hands.

'Are you here for long?'

'Only a few more days, I'm afraid.'

'You're French?'

'Swiss.'

They lit cigarettes and sized each other up.

'You seem to get on very well with Mark and Lucy.'

'I like children.' He glanced sharply at Axley. 'Which is just as well. Mrs Mathews is rather careful whom she trusts, as no doubt you know.'

'That's not our real name,' Lucy piped up suddenly. 'Our real name is Tarnham, but Mummy calls us something else to stop people bothering us.'

Axley smiled at Mournier over the child's head. 'And how old are you, Lucy?'

'Six – but I'll be seven next month. I'm going to get a watch for my birthday and perhaps see Daddy again.'

'You're not supposed to say that, silly!' Mark chipped in. 'It's a secret.'

Lucy burst out crying and then ran off along the beach to where Elissa was drying herself in the sun after her swim.

'Well, she's not!' Mark said belligerently. 'It's a secret. Anyway, Mummy may not be able to get the right watch she wants.'

'When are you going to see your daddy?' asked Axley.

'We don't answer that sort of question, do we, Mark?' Mournier said easily, with a smile at Axley suspiciously like a taunt.

'No,' the boy said obediently. 'We don't answer questions about my father.' It was as if he were giving a Press conference.

'Do you know the father?' Axley asked Mournier.

'Anyone who knew Paul Tarnham would attract a lot of publicity, don't you think? And I'm sure that's the last thing Elissa wants.'

'But you do?'

'I know a lot of people, Major Axley, as you do.'

He was obviously not going to get any further on that tack. The spy stories had all got one important fact in common – you were always out on a limb alone. He searched wildly in his instinct for some clue as to what he should say next. There was no response. An awkward silence followed this last exchange. It was broken by Mournier asking:

'You don't water-ski, Major Axley?'

'I do, as a matter of fact.'

'But not this afternoon?'

Now it was his turn to hedge. 'No – not this afternoon.'

He could see Elissa cosseting her child with Eynsham watching, an almost hungry look on his face. He decided to join them again. Perhaps he could get somewhere with Madame herself. He walked over, followed by Mournier and the boy. To his surprise Elissa received him with a welcoming smile.

'I hear you're a sailing man, Major Axley,' she said. 'Would you feel like giving us a spin this afternoon? Mark and Lucy can put on their lifejackets and I'm a reasonable swimmer.'

'How can you resist such a flattering invitation, Stephen?' Eynsham said. 'She obviously expects you to capsize the boat the moment you step into it.'

'I'd be delighted to,' Axley replied, seeing a new way out. 'I expect Janet would like to come too.'

'Then you must prise her away from Christos.'

'Would you care to join us, sir?' he asked Eynsham. 'There should be room for one more. We shan't be racing.'

'No, thank you, Stephen. I prefer a quiet Sunday afternoon on the sand.'

He watched Elissa and her children following Axley towards the little jetty where the speed-boat was just depositing Janet. On the other side of the pier was a twenty-foot ketch which Axley had been eyeing since they had first come down on the beach. Mournier dropped into the seat vacated by Elissa. There was no one else within earshot of an ordinary conversation.

'I think Major Axley was longing to have the chance of a sail with the wind as it is,' he said. He spoke in an ordinary educated English voice without trace of a French accent. Eynsham looked at him, for a moment or so too astonished to speak.

'Perhaps I could have a few words with you now that we're alone,' Mournier went on, 'if I'm not disturbing your quiet afternoon on the sand.'

'Feel free. I'm all ears.'

'It's a somewhat delicate matter and I don't want to waste your time.'

'You've chosen an odd setting in that case.'

'Oh, I don't know. There are no hidden microphones on this beach. It's of some importance for us not to be overheard. I have a proposition I want to make to you – or a deal, if you like. Ten days ago I was with Paul Tarnham in Prague. In fact he suggested this rather unexpected approach.'

'Who are you?'

'Need we go into all that? I was born in Holland, if it's of any interest, but brought up an Englishman in England – before I was enlightened, shall we say?'

'I don't think I would use that particular word if I can guess what you're going to say.'

The frightening factor was the shock. He felt urgently that he must play for time. But Mournier was not disposed to wait.

'Before you jump to conclusions, let me assure you that we are fully able to honour our side of the deal.' Mournier lit a cigarette and went on: 'We would not be so boorish as to offer a man of your calibre money – though of course there is certainly as much of that in a nice numbered account in Switzerland as you are ever likely to need or to want. We know that you are not basically a money man, so that in your case the consideration we offer is something of much greater value – an embassy of your own.'

'You can fix that?'

'Oh yes. When Harborough returns from London I'm afraid he'll have some rather disappointing news for you – from Stevens. You're being dropped. You'll simply soldier on in the sort of post you're holding down now – and we know how frustrated and bored you find it. But if you consent to work with us then you need pay no attention to Stevens. A new era dawns.'

'Are you solemnly telling me you have that in your gift?'

'Not solemnly but in fact.'

'And if I say no?'

Mournier shrugged his shoulders. 'Then you say no.'

'You're not afraid I'll report this whole fantastic approach?'

'But of course you will.'

'And that doesn't worry you?'

'Why should it? Your report may make a small stir in the servants' hall, shall we say – but naturally it will be taken care of higher up the line.'

'In other words you're telling me you've penetrated the Service right to the top.'

'I'm not telling you anything of the sort. I'm simply offering you a deal which you would be well advised to accept.'

'Provided I can agree to spend the rest of my life a traitor.'

'Oh, these are such old-fashioned words and ideas. "Traitors" and "treachery" – I mean, treachery to what?'

'Well, to one's country for a start.'

'We already know you are not that sort of patriot, Mr Eynsham. You've outgrown it – as indeed have most intelligent people who are concerned for the peace of the world.'

'And how does working for you help that along?'

'Considerably more than working against us. But this is neither the time nor the place for philosophy. I simply want to know now or in the very near future whether you're interested or not. If you are – and I'm sure that you will be if you give it a little thought – then I can assure you you'll be very well taken care of from every point of view.'

By now the shock was numbing. 'I have other problems, you know.'

'We do know them, indeed.'

'And you can take care of them as well?'

Mournier made an impatient gesture. 'This isn't Universal Aunts. We can help – sometimes – at crucial points. Once the decision is made and the will is there, I'm sure you'll find life becomes a whole lot more interesting. Indeed you'll be alive again.'

'Thank you,' Eynsham said sharply. 'I think I know best whether I'm alive or not.' Mournier shrugged his shoulders as if it were of supreme unimportance.

'And what are your bona fides? Apart from your arrogance?' Eynsham went on. A look of surprise flashed across Mournier's face.

'I'm sorry if I strike you as arrogant. I don't think I am, but perhaps it's only because we negotiate from a strong position. We know the facts. We know that what we have to offer will interest you.'

'Even after Philby?'

'Life renews itself, doesn't it, Mr Eynsham? Philby is history. Paul Tarnham, if you like, is history. But today is today. And your services could be invaluable.'

'To the cause of world peace?'

'To the cause of world peace. And let me set your mind at rest on another score. You would not be exposed as Philby was. We don't ever intend asking you to do anything disloyal to England. We are adequately served in that direction. After all' – he paused and looked away into the distance – 'we used to talk about the third man, didn't we? But what about the fourth and the fifth and those whose identity will never be revealed?' He gave a short laugh. 'I don't need to tell an intelligent man like you that Philby was not exactly alone. In any case we are now allies under the skin, so the question of treachery really doesn't arise. But you have American friends and you get on well with the

Chinese. We have some interesting possibilities in those directions.'

'And when do you need to know my answer?'

'Now of course. I don't suppose it is something you want to talk over with the wife, is it?' The idea seemed to give him pleasure and he laughed. Although Eynsham was angry he found Mournier difficult to dislike. He seemed to assume a friendship and take the liberties that went with such a friendship easily in his stride. It was as if he had known Eynsham a long time.

'How much of this does Elissa know?'

'Who knows what goes on inside another's head?' Mournier countered. 'She is a marvellous and intelligent woman, but I would never be able to know what goes on in her head.'

'That was not what I asked.'

'I know,' said Mournier. 'I know what you were asking, but I can't answer it one way or another.'

'I also asked you just now about your bona fides. How do I know you are what you say you are?'

Again the slightly surprised smile. 'But I haven't said I'm anybody, have I? I'm afraid you'll simply have to take me on trust. Although surely I must have convinced you by now that this is not just a game for a Greek Sunday afternoon.'

A silence ensued. By this time Axley had got the ketch in the middle of the bay and Eynsham could just see Elissa and Janet trimming the sails. The rest of the guests were nowhere around. The little beach was deserted. Although the sun was still strong, the loneliness of the place suddenly struck Eynsham with force, and with it the notion of violence or at least of potential violence which almost sprang out of the rocky foreshore. In Greece these days almost anything could be arranged. He turned and studied the young man. Dear God! And Stephen Axley was all they could put up against an operator of this calibre! It was laughable.

'I don't especially wish to talk you into this,' Mournier

went on, 'if indeed I could. The will has to come from you. Knowing how sophisticated you are, I personally have little doubt of the answer – and for what it is worth that is what Paul Tarnham thought too.'

'Did he indeed?'

'Yes, he asked me to say how much he regretted the embarrassment he caused you, but it was hardly unexpected, was it?'

'I don't know what you mean by that, and "embarrassment" is a real Paul Tarnham understatement in view of what happened.'

'Well – I said I'd convey the message.'

'How is he?'

'Paul is fine. Everything worked out for him as intended.'

'Except for Elissa.'

'Perhaps,' Mournier said, following the little yacht in the distance, 'perhaps there are still one or two problems there. But everything is capable of solution.'

Again there was another silence. Shame swirled about inside him in the deep mud of his being and out of which his pride and dignity – or what was left of them – struggled to escape like long distance runners out of a quagmire. With a blend of curiosity and plaintiveness he found himself asking Mournier:

'You do realize to whom you're talking, don't you? – that I am the acting Ambassador for Great Britain, here, at the moment?'

He could easily have exploded with indignation, but as this conventional line sounded ridiculous in his ears when spoken aloud he left the rest unsaid and lapsed into silence.

'I don't know how to answer that,' the younger man said gently, 'except to assure you that your age and position and achievements will be fully respected. We realize that an approach of this kind coming out of the blue like this must inevitably be a shock. However, it is none the less serious for that. Nor is there very much time.'

'Well,' said Eynsham, 'the answer is no – a firm and

unequivocal *no*. And I take it as no compliment to be asked.'

'You are very unwise,' Mournier said tersely, standing up.

'Am I indeed?'

'Do you wish to have longer time?'

'I don't wish to discuss it any further at all.'

'Very well.' The tone was much colder now. 'I'll tell them your decision.'

'You do that,' Eynsham said as the other walked away towards the house, leaving him by himself on the beach.

X

HE WAS now completely alone. The little yacht stood some way out to sea and the speedboat with the water-skiers had gone round the headland. He remained sitting in stillness under the beach umbrella, isolated in both body and thoughts. To whom now could he turn? Whom now could he trust? What was he next to do? To each question a giddy blank presented itself.

He had first to order his thoughts. The British Embassy and life would still go on much as it had before. No one except Mournier and himself knew of the conversation which had just taken place. Or did they? How deeply involved in this approach was Elissa? He shook his head in an attempt to free himself of the shock and the hurt. Everything passes, he told himself, everything passes in time. Yet there was little consolation in that.

He supposed that the shock was mainly to his vanity or pride. That he could be considered as fruitful material for treachery when the image he thought he was projecting was that of Mister Reliable acted on him as a deep depressant. They had considered him as disillusioned and had made the one cynical move open to them. By bringing this out into the light he was thus able to see one of the traps he would need to avoid. They thought him another Tarnham. No doubt Paul had himself fired them with this idea. No doubt Paul thought there was justification for this.

What else did they think of him? That all that mattered was promotion? They were wrong there – or at any rate partially wrong. They had admitted he was not a 'money man' and he was not, in his own eyes, a status seeker to the extent they evidently thought. Your immortal soul for an embassy – it was laughable. Except that both he and they knew perfectly well that his immortal soul did not come into it. Patriotism involving immortal souls had gone out with the barrage balloons, at any rate for him, leaving only personal loyalty and its opposite. Which brought him round once more to Elissa. How much did she really know? Would she abandon her husband now – after three long years – and stay in the West? Above all would she or would she not marry him? In the end everything hinged on Elissa.

The ketch was now sailing back towards the jetty. The afternoon siestas were at an end and there were signs of life in the big house. It was time for him to go. He changed out of his beach clothes and walked up to the terrace. He should normally have waited for Claudia to return from Sounion, but his instinct told him to get out now and send the car back for her later. Several of the other guests were drinking tea, but there was no sign of Jean-Pierre Mournier.

As he reached the foot of the staircase Panayotis Marides came running down, followed by a servant.

'There's been an accident at Sounion – a fall of rock in the cave! We must get out there as quickly as possible!' He ran out, saying: 'Follow me! Bring your own car!'

Marides' Rolls was waiting at the door, and sensibly enough the British Ambassador's car was immediately behind, the driver starting the engine as Rupert got in. It crossed his mind as they set off through a cloud of dust that this was excellent staff work, but he did not dwell on this suspicion for long. He now had an additional weight to carry – a possible accident to Claudia would further complicate his life at this crucial time. Ironically Claudia hale and hearty was far less of a problem than Claudia felled by some accident in a cave. It never rained but it poured. But perhaps she was not involved.

In fact the lower cave to which Claudia, Helen and the professor had penetrated had fallen in and they were trapped. By the time Marides and Rupert arrived, the police were there and local volunteers had begun to dig. Help from the Army had been summoned. No sound could be heard from the inner cave, and the rock had fallen in such a way that they could not get near the previous entrance. It was hot, airless and dark in the outer cave, and they were all hampered by a lack of tools and a lack of space. There was no alternative but to get down to it with their hands.

After half an hour of this they had only penetrated a few feet. Dusk was beginning to fall and there was still no sign of the practical help they needed from the Army.

'I'm going into Athens to raise hell!' Marides said. 'We'll never get anywhere like this. Where are the bull-dozers? Where are the tools? Where's anything? I'm going to have someone's head for this. Thank God I'm British.'

'I'll come with you,' Rupert said and at that moment an Army unit with searchlights and digging tools bustled on to the scene, together with an ambulance. The brisk young officer in charge listened to Marides' explosion of anger for a moment or so and then gave orders to clear all the volunteer workers out of the way. As the real digging began he turned to Marides, who was still aggressively throwing accusations about like squibs at a firework party.

'If you go on like that, Mr Marides,' he said, 'I shall put you under arrest.'

It must have been a long time since anyone had talked to Panayotis Marides in such a way. There was a momentary pause and then he laughed.

'So Greece is now being run by young captains in charge of mechanical shovels! Well, it could get much worse, I suppose.'

'You may be a millionaire,' the young captain said, 'but you do not criticize today in Greece. In a situation like this you simply obey. In this case me. Clear this site!' he called out to his sergeant. 'We're going to blow out the front of the cave.'

As Marides and Eynsham walked away, Marides said:

'They think I'm against the régime if I open my mouth to say boo. Of course I'm not against anyone at all. I'm a business man.'

'Yes,' said Eynsham, but it occurred to him that possibly the Marides had more enemies than they thought. The great millionaire was not perhaps so powerful as he imagined, at all events not in the Greece of today, which for so long from his position of international wealth he had regarded as almost a private estate.

By this time Axley and Janet had arrived from the house. Elissa, they said, was putting the children to bed. A considerable crowd had now gathered to watch the emergency excavation.

'They're at it again in Cyprus,' Axley said in one of the pauses when speech was possible. 'The Turks and the Greeks are brewing up again. It was on the news.'

Eynsham nodded, his thoughts elsewhere. There was always something brewing up in that part of the world. It seemed to him as if the Anglo-Saxon idea of a peaceful life could only be imposed by force, on the Eastern Mediterranean. It was not indigenous. And the Pax Britannica could no longer be forced on anyone anywhere in the world. But what was the strife about? Nothing! Take away the artificially fermented differences and inequalities which always exist between neighbours, and the Greeks and the Turks, like the Arabs and Israelis, would be seen to be what everyone knew them to be – much the same sort of people. But this was a heresy never to be publicly admitted. It was like the division of Ireland, a fifty-year folly, perpetuated by vested interests which were themselves no longer valid, if indeed they ever had been. And in the meantime Claudia lay behind a mass of rubble and stone – possibly dying, possibly dead. He turned his mind away from such thoughts. It either happened or it didn't happen.

'I think I'd better look in at the Embassy', he told Axley, 'if you'll keep an eye on things here. They're going to be some hours yet.'

He was impelled both by a sense of duty and also by a desire to escape for a little time. As the car took him back to Athens he told himself he had had enough for the present. Perhaps, if he were honest with himself, he was running away from a vigil, but he could be back by the time they reached the inner cave, and he needed a break. Enough had already taken place that Sunday for a lengthy digestion.

At the Embassy a Sunday night calm prevailed. The duty officer knew nothing of the trouble in Cyprus, and no one had told him of the disaster at Sounion. Rupert felt like saying that the Chinese had landed an expeditionary force on the Peloponnesus, but he knew the duty officer would only ask if he should draft a telegram that evening or could it wait till morning? He put a call in to Reuters and to the one other correspondent whose judgement he trusted, but could find out nothing of any value except that things were astir. Reluctantly he got back in to the car and drove out to Sounion once more. By this time the Press and the television were there and he had trouble getting through.

Elissa found him in the crowd and squeezed his arm.

'Where's Marides?' he asked.

'Back at the house. He had an urgent call from abroad.'

'And Mournier?' he could not help asking.

She avoided his gaze. 'I expect he's somewhere around. I haven't seen him since we got back from sailing.'

At two in the morning they got them out. Helen Marides was dead, having been killed outright when the fall occurred. Both the professor and Claudia were alive, though unconscious. Claudia's legs were broken, and the professor had internal injuries which had caused him to haemorrhage. Rupert saw her into the hospital where they got to work on her legs, and he then returned home to Kyfyssia. It was 3.30 AM.

At five o'clock in the morning Elissa rang him up. 'I'm scared, Rupert, I don't like it here.'

'What's happened?'

'Nothing, exactly. I just feel afraid. Are you all right?'

'I suppose so. I haven't really taken it all in as yet. Why are you frightened – I mean, especially now?'

'I don't know. There's just a bad feeling in this house. I can't sleep.'

'Are they still up and about?'

'Yes, they are. I'm in the children's room. I think we'll pack up and go back to England tomorrow – I mean, later today. I just feel terribly on edge.'

He had never known her like this. He fought his way back to full consciousness. 'Isn't your friend Mournier around?'

There was no reason why he should be at five o'clock in the morning, but this occurred to him only after he had spoken.

'I think he's gone.'

'Gone where?'

'I don't know. He wasn't here last evening when we got back and I haven't seen him since. Nor any of the other house guests, if it comes to that. There's a great emptiness here.'

He could sense the urgency in her voice. Yet he still drew back. He loved her, but he still found it difficult to trust her.

'Are the children awake?'

'No. It's just me. I'm sorry to wake you up after all you've been through tonight. But I had to talk to someone in the outer world. I mean, outside this house. I wish I'd never come out to Greece. It's all been a big mistake.'

'All of it?'

'Well, not quite all perhaps. Rupert, I think something's going on out here.'

'Something always is,' he answered dryly. 'What especially now?'

'There are a lot of people moving about. I tried to ring you before, but there was always someone on the phone speaking Greek.'

At that moment there was a click and the line went dead. He put the receiver back and lay thinking about it in the darkness for a while. Dawn was beginning to creep into the sky. How many other mornings had he lain like this with Claudia stretched out stiffly beside him, wondering what it was all about, wondering if he would ever be free. It was different now. It reminded him of September 1939, when the Second World War had seemed almost to leak into existence with a kind of dripping uncertainty. Now he had the same feeling in his bones. Doubt swirled around in his mind like an early morning fog. He decided he had better talk to Elissa again and discover what it was all about, but when he rang the line was engaged, and on his trying once more an operator cut in to inform him in English that the number was unobtainable.

By now he was wide awake. Elissa was right. There was something afoot. It looked as if he would need all the energy he could muster to get through the coming day, but as he lay in bed thinking about it he could scarcely steel himself to begin.

Dawn was lighting the sky when Axley rang. 'I'm sorry to disturb you, sir, at this hour of the morning, but there's quite a bit of trouble brewing up. The Turks have closed the border, and there have been something like ten more outbreaks of fighting in Cyprus. I don't know what it's all about as yet, but some new move seems to be under way by our feathered friends.' This was Axley's reference on the open line to the colonel's régime.

'Nothing unusual in that, Stephen,' he said, his mind still on his own troubles ahead.

'No, sir. However, they seem to have arrested Marides.'

'What!'

'And his son as well.'

'I don't suppose you object to that,' he said, playing for time as he tried to think out this extraordinary piece of news. 'Where are you, Stephen?'

'At the Embassy.'

'Good. I'll come in.'

'Shall I send a car for you, sir?'

'No, I'll drive in myself. On second thoughts it might be advisable if we brought in Mrs Mathews and her children.'

'That's just what I was thinking, sir.'

'So you'd better have an official car standing by.'

'Would you like me to go out and get them?'

He thought about this and decided that Axley might not have the authority to bluster his way through the obstructionism which he could well encounter at the Marides establishment.

'I think this is a job for both of us. I'll meet you there – no, wait a minute – I'll come round by the Embassy and we'll go out together in the ambassadorial barouche. Have they got the tanks out again?'

'No, sir, everything is apparently peace and quiet.'

'Have you drafted a situation report for London?'

'Yes. It will be waiting for you here.'

He dressed and drove in to Athens, trying to work out the implications. The colonels must be very sure of themselves if they went for someone as powerful as Panayotis Marides. The Turkish border dispute though apparently serious was more likely to be a cover for some other move, perhaps one which had already gone wrong. Were they in fact, behind the scenes, working exactly counter to their carefully fostered image? Was it the Eastern bloc they were after and in which Marides evidently had a substantial part to play? If so, what had gone wrong? The house yesterday had been full of Chinese and Eastern diplomats. The more he thought about it, the more sure he became that Marides was the key to this situation and that some closer relationship with Communism had at least been mooted. In which case what had misfired? A familiar chill somewhere near the kidneys reminded him of Mournier's approach to himself the previous afternoon. Perhaps there were plural keys – Marides being one and himself another. It was not an agreeable thought.

It was just as well that they drove out in the ambassadorial car. Checkpoints had sprung up along the road past Vouliagmeni, manned by self-important police.

'What's the show in aid of?' Axley asked, but this was a rhetorical question. The unnecessary display of power was yet another outward mark of the dictatorship to which Greece was becoming daily more and more accustomed. The shouting and the strutting had taken root. But the stony-faced pair in the Embassy car paid no attention. Eynsham assumed, as did any diplomat of his experience, that in times of crisis the Corps Diplomatique is more than a match for the lower echelons of the police. If there was rudeness or reluctance to observe the amenities he simply drove on, knowing the police of that grade would not fire on a diplomatic car. Thus they got through to the house itself.

Here they found a different situation. A small detachment of the Security Police guarded the house, and at first they were refused admittance. Then, when Eynsham insisted on seeing the officer in charge, there was another delay and they were suddenly ushered inside. In the familiar hall which he seemed to have left only a few minutes ago, Eynsham found himself face to face with Lambakis, arrayed as before in dark glasses, looking even at that hour of the morning like a knowledgeable toad.

'We are making a little investigation,' he said blandly, offering his hand to Rupert.

'Where is Mr Marides?'

'He and his son are both helping the police with their inquiries, as you so tactfully put it in England.'

'You realize Marides is a British subject with a British passport?'

'But not, I hope, of Asian extraction – or he might have difficulty in exercising his rights – isn't that so? Yes, we are fully aware of Mr Marides' connexions. Indeed that is why we are here.'

Rupert tried to penetrate the barrier of the dark glasses and once again failed.

'Well, I suppose you know what you are doing,' he said after a pause, 'and the dangers you may run into.'

'Oh yes, Mr Eynsham, but do you?'

'That's a somewhat offensive remark to an ambassador.'

'You are in Greece,' the other said with sudden controlled force, 'and you are talking to a Greek. We are no longer in need of imperialist advice, Mr Eynsham, as your country has found out elsewhere in the world.'

'Are you going to help Greece in the way you once helped Peron?' Eynsham said with icy incision. 'How fortunate Greece is to have men of your calibre at her disposal.'

The other froze into complete stillness for a moment or so. The three men, Eynsham, Axley and the toad, stood at the foot of the stairs watched by three gorilla-type Security Police.

'Thank you for your compliments. I will see they reach the right quarters. However, if I may advise the Acting Ambassador of Great Britain, liberties should not be taken with the Greek Security Police.' He paused slightly and relaxed his tone. 'Now, Mr Eynsham, what can I do for you? I was so sorry to hear of Mrs Eynsham's accident yesterday.' The touch of acid had returned to his voice and his self-control seemed more formidable than ever.

'I should like to talk to Mrs Mathews, please.'

'Ah, now that might be difficult. She's no longer here.'

'She was an hour ago. I talked to her on the telephone.'

'I dare say you did' – Lambakis was now taking no trouble to disguise his insolence – 'but since then she and her two children hurriedly packed, called for a taxi and left. We put no difficulties in her way. Greece is a free country and people can come and go as they like.'

'Do you know where she went?'

Lambakis gave an eloquently negative shrug of the

shoulders. 'Perhaps to the airport – but of course that is closed because of the Turkish trouble – perhaps to an Athens hotel. I'm so sorry you've come all this way for nothing.'

'Do you mind if I have a look upstairs?' Axley said, moving to the stairs.

Lambakis jerked his head at two of the gorillas, who moved at once to bar the way.

'You are surely not doubting my word, are you, Major Axley?'

'Of course not, Mr Lambakis,' Axley replied with unexpected sang-froid. 'I simply wished to go upstairs. Both the Ambassador and I were guests yesterday, under happier circumstances.'

'May I ask why you wish to go upstairs?'

'You may ask but you won't get a reply.' Axley was keeping control of himself, but only with difficulty. Lambakis looked at him with his insincere smile.

'I take it then that you have no further business here. So I must ask you both to leave.'

Without a word Eynsham turned and strode to the door, followed by Axley. As they drove back to the Embassy Axley remarked:

'I think he was speaking the truth.'

'You mean about Greece being a free country?' Eynsham said wryly.

'I don't think they were in the house. They've cleared everyone out. I think Lambakis is going to tear the whole place apart.'

'I wonder who it is Marides has omitted to pay,' Eynsham said as he thought it out. 'I don't suppose Christos will enjoy a going-over by the Security boys either. We'll call in at the airport and see if she's there. My guess is she'll have gone to an hotel.'

XI

BY THE time Janet came in to the Embassy to begin yet another Monday, the Turco-Greek crisis was clattering to a familiar climax. As usual the Greeks in Cyprus, cheating along the inside edge of an agreement, had slipped in an illegal saturation of troops. Equally as usual the Turks were not going to allow themselves to be provoked beyond a certain point. It was the classic pattern. So on that Monday morning when Claudia lay in hospital unconscious with her legs in plaster, and a couple of broken ribs, when both Marides and his son had been put away into solitary confinement in the grim security prison, the Cypriot mixture had again been brought to explosion point, the borders were closed and the usual paraphernalia of needless, self-destructive, self-manufactured crisis lay littered about the Athenian scene.

'The hell of it is that we've got to take it seriously,' Axley remarked to Janet as he waited to see the Counsellor. 'Like the dolly drops, the time comes sooner or later when the overdose is for real.'

'What time did the Counsellor get to bed?'

'After three AM, and I had him up at six.' Janet took off her coat and sat at her desk. 'What's the word on Mrs Eynsham?'

'She'll live.'

'It's awful to say it,' said Janet, 'but what a solution that would have been.'

'Yes. What are we going to do with Elissa and the children?'

'I don't get you, Stephen. What do you mean – what are *we* going to do?'

'They're here in the Embassy now. Up in the visitors' suite.'

'*Here?* Why? Did Marides throw them out?'

'The Marides are in no position to throw anyone out. The gorillas have got them.'

He told her what had happened during the night.

'So Elissa and the children came here themselves. They tried to get on a plane for London but the airport is closed.'

'Do you mean to say those bloody thugs took in Marides five minutes after his wife was killed?'

'I don't suppose they were thinking of that.'

'Aren't they human? She was still his wife and the mother of Christos.'

'It's possible the accident in the cave really was an accident. In which case it may have forced them to act somewhat ahead of time.'

'Good heavens!' Janet said, thinking this out. 'If it wasn't an accident, why on earth would they have wanted to get rid of Helen Marides?'

'I don't think it was Helen Marides they were after. But with Mrs Eynsham out of it – that might have opened the way to other things. In any case the Marides would hold the key. And the Marides must suddenly have fallen from grace. Not that Christos is any personal loss. But why? And what's happened to Jean-Pierre Mournier? He could program the computer too. At least that's my guess – he and old man Panayotis.'

'I wonder they dared.'

'I don't. This lot is far more powerful behind the scenes than anyone thinks. Of course it may just be that one of the colonels wants to get his hands on the Marides estates in Greece. In which case send for the Tontons Macoutes. Mr Teroutanian Lambakis found his way around under Peron in the Argentine. He'll have a trick or two up his sleeve.'

'He sounds like the local Beria.'

'He could be at that. He certainly knows what he's doing all right.'

The telephone buzzed on her desk.

'All right, Stephen, the Counsellor will see you now.'

Eynsham looked in good shape considering the night he had just been through.

'H.E.'s going to New York to the Security Council meeting. So we're on our own a while longer. Keep an eye on our problem children – I must go and see how Claudia's getting on.'

'Are they under house arrest?'

'Why should they be?'

'Suppose they want to go out?'

'I doubt very much if Elissa will want to go to the beach at a time like this.'

'But if she does?'

'Let her. We've no powers to stop her. She's asked for sanctuary until the planes start flying again. She's hardly likely to want to go out shopping. Not at this level of crisis.'

'That may be a little time. The Turks have threatened to invade Cyprus if the Greek element isn't withdrawn from the UN demarcation area by midnight tonight.'

'They'll withdraw. The colonels know what would happen if the Turks let them have it. And the Turks are aching to do it.'

'In the meantime we have this unexploded bomb and her two bomblets in the Embassy.'

'You don't think much of her, do you, Stephen?'

'Yes I do.' But he could not keep the doubt out of his voice. 'It's just that we have more than enough on our plate at the present. I have a feeling that they haven't played their trump card as yet.'

'Haven't they?' Eynsham said, thinking of yesterday afternoon.

'I can't see them bringing Madame and her family all the way out here just so that her host and his son can be arrested. There's another element in it – somewhere.'

'Such as?'

Axley hesitated. It obviously cost him an effort to talk like this. 'I think they may well make some sort of direct approach to you, sir, if you'll excuse my saying so – because of the Tarnham connexion. A fairly high-powered approach made by someone who hasn't yet shown his hand. Or someone brought here on purpose.'

Eynsham smiled. He was exhausted and the day had hardly begun. Yet here was this polite, sensitive young man warning him about something which had already taken place, something which his superiors had worked out as quite likely to happen.

'You mean I'm on the list for recruitment?'

'I'm not trying to be insulting, sir, but yes: I imagine you are.'

'And what would you advise me to do in such an event?'

'Show interest and let us know.'

'Us?'

'Well, me, then and I'll pass it on.'

He studied Axley's face, trying to decide how much he knew, how innocent he really was. If Mournier's claim yesterday had had any truth in it, this stiff and formal young man might also be part of the trap. Who indeed was to be trusted in this post-Philby age?

'I'm going to the hospital to see how Claudia is. I'll be back as soon as I can.'

'If the Greeks and the Turks have a war, what happens to us?' Mark asked his mother. They were sitting in the guest suite at the Embassy bored to distraction. Lucy had been given paper and pencil for drawing and a Robert Louis Stevenson had been produced from the Embassy library for Mark. But outside the early summer day shouted to them to come down to the beach, and both children had been puzzled and frightened by their sudden departure from the Marides' house in the middle of the night.

'We must try and get away,' Elissa said, 'but at least we're safe here for the present.'

'Are we going to join Father in Russia?'

'I don't think so, Mark. In any case we'll go back to London first.'

'Oh!'

He was a hard, tough little boy, she thought, very like his father and just as locked away in himself. The bond between father and son had become stronger instead of weaker during the last three years. He was very much his father's boy and she found herself unwillingly resentful of this.

'I like Uncle Rupert,' Lucy said, absorbed in her drawing.

'He's not your uncle, silly. He's just a friend of Mummy's.'

'And you don't, Mark, do you?' Elissa asked.

As always he avoided her gaze. 'Not very much. I don't mind him a lot.'

'Well, I'm very fond of him and he's been very helpful to us.'

'Do you want to marry him instead of Father?' Mark asked, pretending to be sunk in his book but looking up at her slyly.

She thought about this for a moment or so. 'I might,' she said.

'Is that why he got into bed with you the other night?'

She looked steadily at his averted face. It always came at you when least expected.

'Yes, Mark, that's part of the reason. I didn't know you were awake. You had no business peeping.'

'I didn't for long. He got out and started to dress so I went back to bed. He has funny knees, hasn't he?'

'I didn't notice his knees,' she said, and laughed. The conversation was absurd. She had felt so hot and bothered about it at the time in case the children knew and were shocked. When it happened it seemed the most ordinary thing in the world. Then Lucy took her side.

'Why shouldn't he get into bed with Mummy if he wants to? We do.'

'He's not our father,' Mark said stubbornly.

'No,' Elissa said firmly, 'and if your father showed up now I very much doubt if I'd let him either.'

'Well, I'd like to go and see him in Russia.'

'And never come back?'

Mark pretended not to hear and turned away. He could be very mulish at times.

'Come on, Lucy,' Elissa said. 'I'll play you a game of Chinese patience.'

Later in the morning Axley asked if he could see her for a few minutes.

'I really don't want another interrogation. I've been up half the night,' she told Janet, 'and the children are difficult enough as it is.'

'They can play in the garden. It's quite safe there. It's only a few questions about the Marides, I think.'

She agreed in the end, and a little later Axley arrived with the false confidence of someone who might set about selling her cut-price insurance. She suddenly saw what it was.

'I believe you're more scared of this than I am,' she said. 'Don't you like security work?' This made him smile.

'Am I that bad? Or rather obvious?'

'Not at all. You're rather nice, I think. You just don't seem to fancy your work very much.'

'I'll level with you,' Axley said. 'I detest it but in return for that will you tell me a thing or two about the Marides?'

'I can try.'

'How well did your husband know Panayotis when you were in Greece before?'

'I never knew how well Paul got on with anyone – and that's the truth. I used to think I knew, but his abrupt departure shattered all that. I suppose the short answer is, well enough to ask Pan to be godfather to Mark.'

'Do you think Marides is a Communist?'

She laughed. 'You certainly take the bull by the horns, don't you? I should think he's everything, wouldn't you? He's a business man. I fancy he carries a credit card for every political faction there is from far right to far left. He might even be a middle of the road Conservative.'

'Why do you think they've arrested him?'

'Because the people who run Greece at the moment are abysmally vain, greedy and stupid.'

'But surely he was hand in glove with the régime?'

'That's what one would imply. I mean, how else could he behave as he did? But I really know nothing about his political connexions. As to why he's been arrested – I suppose possession is nine-tenths of the law, even in Greece. No doubt he has a lot they want to get their hands on. All right, so now they've got him. Where do you go from there?'

'Can you tell me anything about Jean-Pierre Mournier?'

'Nothing I'm sure you don't know already. He's a link man. He's been in touch with Paul in Russia.'

'Ah!'

'You seem surprised.'

'Only to hear you say it at last.'

'Listen, Major Axley,' she said crisply. 'I've been gone over by experts. In the three years since Paul went I've suffered almost every form of interrogation there is. Your people have known Paul's whereabouts all along. I don't know why you're playing this game. Or are these walls bugged and are you trying to lead me on in some way? I've nothing new to tell you. I'm really fed up with it all. I just want to get back to England as soon as I can.'

For once Axley showed traces of anger too. 'This isn't a game, Mrs Tarnham, and you aren't the only person to have been up all night. We may find ourselves in the middle of a war at any moment – right here in Athens. You've been in touch with your husband for three years and it was part of a plan that you came to Greece. Can you tell me why?'

'No.'

She stared at him coldly. Neither said anything for a moment or so. He was quite unable to decide if the 'No' meant she was refusing or simply did not know.

'No you can't or no you won't?'

'Just simply no.' There was another pause, then she said: 'I'm not being antagonistic as you seem to think. I've just had my fill of it all. I want out – if you like.'

'Unfortunately you can't have "out" just like that – and you know it. The situation remains – and we have to cope with it.'

'What situation, for heaven's sake? I don't want to be rude, but where's your sense of proportion? I'm not a female James Bond and you and your people know it. I don't see how you expect me to help.'

'I think you could help a great deal if you were minded to do so.'

'How?'

'By being considerably more forthcoming.'

'I don't understand.'

'Oh yes you do. Something was going to happen out here, wasn't it? And it hasn't. Something's gone wrong with the timing. Isn't that so?'

She smiled without showing a trace of the nervousness and the pressure she felt.

'I don't know what you're talking about, and since you seem to be answering the questions you're asking, Major Axley, you really leave me nothing to say.'

By the evening it seemed impossible that war between Greece and Turkey could be avoided. The usual pattern of events was taking place. The American President's special envoy was shuttling between Ankara and Athens, the Security Council had met but had so far not pronounced, and the British Prime Minister was exhorting both sides and borrowing a little ready cash to bolster up the pound.

'Our contribution to any crisis these days', Rupert said to Elissa over a drink, 'seems to be to lecture the Americans about Vietnam and leave the brinkmanship to those on the spot.'

He had now been on the go for what seemed like a week, and this was a hurried five minutes snatched between meetings.

'You always wanted an embassy of your own, Rupert – now you seem to have got one by accident.'

'The little man gets back tomorrow. Direct from New York.'

'If he can fly in why can't I fly out?'

'Maybe you will. Just at present, though, civilians can wait – say the Greeks. And the tanks have reappeared round Athens so they're taking no chances.'

'What's H.E. going to say when he finds me installed?'

'Blame me, I should think, and check the level of the whisky decanter.'

'The children are fretting. They hate being cooped up here after the Marides' beach. I'm not complaining, Rupert. We're very grateful and all that but it would be nice to get away, and Mark keeps wanting to see his father. I've failed to sell you to the children as a substitute.'

'To hell with the children. What about you?'

'That's different.' She went over and kissed him. 'See?' she said. 'The years drop away from your tired old face.'

'Do that again and see if we can get back to childhood.'

'You're a growing habit,' she said. 'I might well be getting hooked.'

'Stay that way till I get back from the next session at the Greek Foreign Office. If I'm not carried out asleep.'

XII

WHEN at last he got to bed in the Embassy, he was scarcely allowed to sleep. Foreign Office telegrams arrived in a continuous stream, and most of the Embassy staff had come in to lend a hand or simply be around. It was like the war, and Rupert had to delve into his memory for an endurance test of such length and intensity.

'And it must have been nicely ironic to have Madame a few doors up the corridor but still inaccessible,' Axley said snidely to Janet in the morning as she tidied the office and prepared for another crisis day.

She gave him a sharp look. 'I think you rather fancy her yourself.'

'I do – out of the Embassy and preferably away from Greece.'

'I see they've got the tanks out again. I thought it was the Turks they were supposed to be worried about. The Turks are not going to drop out of the sky on Athens, are they?'

'The Greeks are always worried about the Turks – and with good reason. They had them sitting on their necks for five hundred years. They know what they're like. However, I think this whole crisis is a convenient cover plan for some in-fighting among the colonels themselves. That's where it really is and that's why the tanks are out.'

The phone rang and Janet took down a message.

'Just to help the Counsellor get started,' she said, 'the news from the hospital is that Mrs Eynsham has shock complications and they'd like him to come along as soon as possible.'

It was a grey, broody day – unusual for Athens at that time of year – but appropriate, Rupert felt, as he drove to see Claudia. The problem was to keep his head above it all. At such times it was necessary to hold on to something firm in himself. Like a religion, for example, which he did not have. Apply the Sebastian Bannister technique, he told himself, and this memory took him back to an earlier day when Sebastian Bannister had been a larger-than-life ambassador of the old school on whom Rupert had modelled his behaviour as a junior member of the Foreign Service in pre-war China. Watch and wait, do nothing whenever possible, since whatever you do is likely to be wrong – praise the Lord and pass on the paper work – and above all, my boy, remember that it's what you *are* in yourself that matters, not *who* you are, nor what you *do*, but what your quality is. The picture of the tall Edwardian with his moustache and his elegant clothes, his feet up on the ambassadorial desk while his embassy was under siege and out of communication with the world came vividly to Rupert's mind as he tried to think a present way through the crisis ahead. The tougher it got the more apparently relaxed S. Bannister became, and this image had stood Rupert in good stead from then on.

Claudia was only partially conscious. She had a poor colour and gave a generally disturbing impression. Rupert kissed her on the cheek and felt her eyes glueing on to him.

'The bad night's over, Claudia.'

'No,' she whispered, 'it's only just begun. Rupert, if anything happens to me—'

'Nonsense,' he said firmly. 'You're going to be all right.'

She paid no attention and this brought home to him how really ill she must be.

'You'd better take on Elissa and have done with it.' She closed her eyes for a moment and then went on: 'She won't do you any good – but if that's what you want, do it before it's too late.'

'You're going to be all right,' he said lamely, but there was no response. It was beginning to look as if she might not be all right at all.

'It's not only my legs,' she murmured after a pause, 'there's something wrong inside. I've been bleeding in the night.'

For the first time in years he felt a compassion. The day's problems continued to claw at him, yet here was a timelessness and a reality which forced them to hold off for a while. He looked down at her white face, those sharp beaky features which had for so long dominated his life, the wrinkled hands, the wispy hair. The lovelessness of it all appalled him. She looked so forlorn. He took hold of her hand and was astonished to find the tears springing to his eyes. Why had he not been able to love her to her needs? Why in her turn had she never given him a single thing he had wanted?

'In any case,' she went on quietly, her eyes half closed, 'I think I'll go back to England: put Pojo in quarantine for six months and go and live with Charles.'

Charles was her brother, a retired tea planter who had reverted to Tunbridge Wells. On the few occasions Rupert had met him he had seemed as solitary as his sister. Perhaps they needed each other more than he and Claudia did. Perhaps that was the answer. He did not argue the point with himself.

'The first thing is to get you well again.'

He could not even make his tone of voice sound convincing. She was in a bad way and both of them knew it. The doctor and nurse came and turned him out. They told him there was injury to both liver and kidneys which was not responding to treatment.

'On top of the damage to her legs, the shock is considerable,' the doctor told him as he walked to the car. 'Also the will to recover doesn't seem to be there. There will be another climax to come – perhaps in a matter of hours. But she does not seem to want to live.' The doctor shrugged his shoulders and looked sideways at Rupert. 'It sometimes happens that ladies of that age take no further pleasure in life. Then when a disaster such as this arrives they have no reserves. Let us hope for the best.'

He sped back to the Embassy past the menacing clumps of soldiers which had now come out like a rash all over Athens. No sooner had he got to his desk than Axley came to see him. He wore what he fancied to be his enigmatic expression.

'Lambakis has been shot.'

'Has he now?' Rupert took his time absorbing this astonishing piece of news. 'Taken and shot – or murdered?'

'Murdered. In bed, as a matter of fact. Coincidentally the Marides – father and son – have stopped helping the police with their inquiries and were both released after breakfast. The report I have is that the son is somewhat the worse for wear; Panayotis, I hear, is just very, very angry.'

'Has he gone back to the house?'

'Yes. There's his wife's funeral to be seen to – among other pressing things. The yacht has been ordered here – if the message gets through.'

'It'll get through. I can't think why he didn't have it all the time.'

'It was undergoing a refit.'

'Where?'

'In a Rumanian shipyard, I think. Or it may just have been Istanbul.'

'Find out. It might be important. It could well be that Marides and Lambakis were trying to work on the régime from opposite sides, Marides from the Eastern bloc, Lambakis – well, I don't know what faction he'd represent – but certainly not democracy.'

'I think he was aiming at a take-over bid at the top.'

'He was that ambitious?'

Axley nodded. 'From what we know of the present infrastructure, a man of parts such as Lambakis could have tried – in fact did set the gang one against another – to blackmail his way into a controlling position.'

'You could be right,' Rupert said thoughtfully. 'Lambakis did his homework under Peron. Do we know who murdered him?'

'No, but I can guess who caused it to happen.'

'Yes, Stephen, so can I.' He worked out some of the implications of this. 'But even from prison?'

'Just because he was put in prison, I imagine. He couldn't operate as he did without taking certain precautions. What man of Marides' power would expose himself in Greece today without making protective arrangements in certain obvious events? I think that plan went into action the moment Marides was arrested. Lambakis was killed and the Marides promptly released.'

'Murder is a sizeable protective arrangement to make.'

'Yes, but Lambakis may well have had exactly the same thing in mind himself and Marides knew this – perhaps. No dictator ever quailed at knocking off a few hot competitors near the top of the ladder. Once Lambakis had got his hands well into the moneybags, it's quite possible Marides himself and his son would have been knocked off – pseudo-legally of course – before international pressure for his release became too embarrassing.'

'All right, Stephen, you'd better let me have an official note of all this for the Ambassador to see on his return.'

As Axley left the room Janet came in to say:

'Mr Marides is here and wants to see you at once. You're due at the American Embassy in twenty minutes' time. Will you see him?'

'I certainly will. Show him in straight away.'

There was no doubt Marides was in a rage, but it took a dangerously quiet form. The exuberance, the flash certainty, the flamboyance were gone. Instead there was an exhausted but wary man who had obviously been through an ordeal and who was battling with shock.

'I've come for Elissa.'

'I'm not sure she'll want to go back with you, but I'll get her down and ask.' Rupert was aware that Marides' attitude had changed for the colder, even though it had never been especially close. It was not difficult to dislike Marides. However, he still made an attempt at politeness.

'How is Mrs Eynsham?'

'Not very well, I'm afraid. There are complications. Do you need any help over your wife's funeral arrangements?'

'What sort of help? The only sort of help I need is here.' And he tapped his chest firmly.

'Are you going to complain about your treatment?'

'Complain? Why should I? I volunteered to help of my own accord. There were misunderstandings, that's all. I have nothing to complain about.'

'You weren't arrested? That was certainly the idea I had from Lambakis.'

'Ah! I cannot speak for Lambakis. And I did not come here to talk about that.'

Rupert suddenly felt short-tempered with this aggressive and unpleasant man standing in his office and telling him what to do. There was no monopoly in shock and exhaustion. He called in Janet.

'Take Mr Marides to the visitors' room and ask Elissa to see him. Is the car waiting?' She nodded. 'Right, then I'm on my way. I'm sorry to be unable to offer you what you want, Mr Marides. However, you have only to ask.'

'I don't know what you're talking about; but there are certainly many ways to help, some of which I think you know.'

Rupert countered the Greek's hard, calculating look by saying quietly:

'And I in turn have no idea what you are talking about. If you want help from us here, you must be explicit. So far as I am concerned you were arrested and your house searched. If you choose now for reasons of your own to describe this as a voluntary action on your part – that's up to you. But don't distort the facts for my benefit. We are not under threat in this Embassy.'

'Who's talking about threats? You are confusing that manufactured situation out there in the streets with the realities you and I both know perfectly well. We both know window dressing when we see it. We both know that barring accidents – and on the best terms to be had – a détente *will* be arranged between Turkey and Greece. And you personally know, my friend, where that area is in which you can be of growing use to the cause of peace and at the same time benefit yourself.'

The door closed behind him as he followed Janet out. Rupert was left for the moment astonished at the nerve of the man, pausing also to reflect that Marides must have been fully aware of the proposition put to him on Sunday by Jean-Pierre Mournier. Dodging about in his mind as well was the uneasy idea that murder must have been calculated, organized and employed in some process he did not comprehend to re-establish the Greek in his previous position of power.

With Elissa Marides came straight to the point.

'I've come to take you and the children back. How soon

can you be packed?' It was obvious that at least one layer of polish had been stripped away.

She played it back cautiously and coolly. 'How marvellous they let you out. How did you fix it?'

'It was a misunderstanding.'

'The whole thing? The searching of the house and all that?'

Marides was impatient. 'Everything. A misunderstanding. Now we put all that behind us and we get on with the life.'

'What about Helen's funeral?'

'Tomorrow. You can help straighten things up. Christos will need a few days' rest. He caught something infectious at the interrogation centre. He's not well.'

'You mean they beat him up?'

'I mean he needs a few days to recover, whereas I have a lot to do. The day after tomorrow I'm supposed to be in Bucharest and then Tokyo.'

She gave him a careful look. 'I think now we're installed in the Embassy, we'll stay here until we can fly back to London – which will be as soon as the airport's open and things are normal again.'

'Well, *I* think it would be better if you came home with me.'

She paused for a moment, assessing the compulsion in his voice.

'The crisis—' she began.

'Crisis! crisis! There *is* no crisis. A lot of bloody Greeks and Turks glaring at each other across a road. There's no crisis. All that is for the Press. The fixing of a charter for my 150,000-ton tanker at Hamburg: that's a crisis all right when you can't get through on the telephone. First things first, Elissa. Now you pack your things and come home with me.'

'No, thank you. Not as things are.'

She realized he was very angry indeed. 'I can't force you, Elissa, but I should very much like you to come. Quite apart from the fact that you are here at my invitation and expense.'

'Thank you for reminding me of that. I hadn't forgotten.' She looked straight back into his glaring eyes. 'And we've had a lovely time – if not perhaps as quiet as we'd expected. But all things come to an end.'

'The matter you came for has not yet been settled.'

'Which particular matter?'

'You're being obtuse and difficult.'

'Yes, possibly I am – but then I've learnt it from you. And I'll tell you why. I didn't realize till I came out here what a violent country this is – nor how involved with it you are.'

'Good God, I *am* Greek.'

'You have British nationality. You live in four or five different countries. You may look on yourself as Greek – but you're Greek with a difference.'

'Of course I'm a Greek with a difference. To begin with I'm a multimillionaire. Now please be reasonable. What can possibly happen to you now?'

'I don't know,' she said unhappily. 'Did you foresee what has just happened to you?'

'I was aware of the possibility,' he said quietly. 'I took one or two essential precautions.'

'I'm sorry. As things are I'd rather the children and I stayed on here in the Embassy.'

Without another word he turned abruptly and left the room. She shivered. Upstairs Lucy began to cry. She walked slowly up to see what it was all about, torn and uncertain in herself.

'Mark twisted my arm! He won't let me play with his Action Man!'

She straightened out that little problem and then sat over by the window looking down on the Embassy garden. Panayotis was right – the matter she had come out to Greece to decide was still unsettled. Should she go or stay? Would she ever find out the answer this way? The rain that was so unusual at that time of year continued to fall in a steady drizzle.

XIII

ALMOST exactly as Marides had forecast, the tension between Turkey and Greece began to relax that afternoon with the withdrawal of the Greek troops. Tanks and soldiers disappeared from the Athens street corners as suddenly as they had arrived. Normal communications were re-established, and by the time the Ambassador returned from New York it was as if the events of the last few days had never taken place.

Rupert would normally have gone to the airport, but the hospital called him to say that Claudia was in a critical state. So Axley met the Ambassador. In the car on the way to the Embassy he gave him a run-down on the events of the last few days. Harborough did nothing to hide his impatience.

'Do you mean to say that that woman and her children are cluttering up the Embassy?'

'It was an emergency, sir.'

'It won't be once I get back in the saddle.' James Harborough always talked as if the cavalier outlook derived from an almost daily equestrian experience. In fact he had never been on a horse in his life.

'Why couldn't she have gone back home?' he went on. 'We have enough problems as it is without a new Tarnham complex.'

'It happened early in the morning. She needed help.' Axley tried to keep his own contempt for the Ambassador out of his voice but only partially disguised it. 'Marides had been arrested. Lambakis was very much in the ascendant. I think it was a wise move to have made at the time. None of us knew what lay ahead.'

'Has the Counsellor—' The Ambassador hesitated, searching for a tactful way of asking what Axley knew he wanted to find out. 'Have there been any repercussions?'

The possible answers to this question nearly made Axley laugh aloud.

'I don't quite get what you mean, sir.'

'From the other side of course.'

'None as yet.'

'Don't you think that there will be?'

'I doubt it. The timing seems to have gone wrong. Lambakis got Marides out of the way at what may have been a crucial moment.'

'You think Marides is the link with Tarnham now?'

'Probably. But I don't know what's gone wrong. Jean-Pierre Mournier seems to have disappeared as well. He was the one who had met Paul Tarnham in Prague. He'd suggested to the children that they might soon be seeing their father.'

'I can't think why she doesn't take them across and have done with it.'

'Provided she doesn't take anyone else with her as well.'

The Ambassador looked sideways at his military attaché.

'Do you consider there's a danger of that?'

There was a long pause as Axley thought out the implications behind the question.

'There's a possibility, of course – but I wouldn't put it higher than that. Other factors come into it about which I have no knowledge.'

'Such as?'

'Well, promotion for one thing. That might affect a decision.'

'Yes,' said the Ambassador, staring straight ahead into space; 'that's something in the lap of the gods for all of us.'

Claudia died at 4.30 the following morning. She regained a moment or two of consciousness just after midnight, murmured a few incoherent words about Pojo, her dog, and then lapsed into the void for ever. Rupert stayed with her holding her hand, his brain surprisingly active, his thoughts going back over their life together, his own consciousness probing the unknown with questions to which there were never direct answers and perhaps never any answers, as such, at all. He wondered if the mystery had been revealed to Claudia before she died. He seemed at times like this to be able to separate from himself, almost to stand outside himself and watch it all going on. He was aware that a period of numbness and shock would soon be upon him – but at the moment the brilliance of that energy which comes from a second wind illuminated his mind.

For a few short moments he saw how it was. He saw the essential loneliness of Claudia both unreachable and incurable when she was alive and now cured for ever. He saw himself equally lost. He saw Elissa at first striding confidently into the darkness of the forest and then beginning to falter and grope. They were each of them, in a different way, aware of the unknown, each of them animated by private fears they would never reveal. With Claudia it had been the terror of sex, her timid spirit being stained and shut in with the full load of Victorian superstition which her recessive upbringing had forced upon her. With Elissa it was the solitary responsibility of being both mother and father, having an apparent freedom of choice which in reality was no more than a fancy illusion. With himself – what now? What sort of person had been brought to this point by the passage of life? Was he really the coward he suspected himself of being? Looking down on his dead wife and the childless aridity of their marriage, he asked, as he had asked countless times before, what was the point of his life. What had he achieved other than just keeping himself alive? He saw despair, that gaunt familiar figure lurking in the shadows, waiting for the present light to dim. Strangely enough it seemed to him now to have the features of James Harborough, Her Britannic Majesty's Ambassador to Greece. With a last look at Claudia, now white, peaceful and slightly smiling, he left the hospital and drove home through the dawn.

'Now that the crisis is over, you should have no difficulty in getting your booking,' Harborough said to Elissa when he sent for her on his return. 'Of course you're most welcome to stay as long as is necessary.'

'You mean you'd like me to get out as soon as I can?'

'I've not yet talked to Rupert, so I don't yet know on what basis you were provided with Embassy hospitality. We have other guests arriving, of course.'

She gave him a smouldering look. 'May I ask why you dislike me so much? What have I done to you?'

'I don't know what you're talking about,' Harborough said stiffly. 'We were merely discussing your accommodation in my Embassy.'

'Very well. We'll go to an hotel tonight.'

'There is no need for that. You may certainly stay till tomorrow. I was merely observing that the exceptional circumstances of the crisis are now over.'

'And your Embassy is not to be used for waifs and strays. I quite see that.'

She was so angry she decided she would ring up Panayotis and go back to the big house in spite of her misgivings. When she regained her room, however, the wisdom of not doing anything drastic in anger came back to her and she settled for another night of inactivity. The children, however, were nearly distracted with boredom. The following day come what may they must make a move.

After four hours' sleep Rupert got up, had a bath and made himself some coffee. There had been no sign of Eudoxia. She had not appeared the day before, and he concluded with relief that she must have been part of the Lambakis faction. That was one problem the less. He wondered in passing who was now filling the vacuum left by yesterday's murder. With one of the pretenders out of the way, there would be gaps all over the fabric.

He drove in to the Embassy through the hot, clear summer morning. Exhausted though he was, confused as he might be about the future, he reacted with a leap of joy in his heart to the exhilaration, the light and the colour of Greece. The storm and the stress of the last few days, the uncertainties ahead – all were forgotten in that short morning drive from Kyfyssia with the bougainvillea shouting its purple song from every wall. Greece was at times so lovely and so moving a country, it brought a lump to his throat. Even the Greeks were bearable on a day like this.

When he reached the Embassy the atmosphere of an English country house on a quiet weekend had once more been restored. The rumbling crisis they had just been through might well have taken place in the previous decade instead of the day before. Janet was at her desk – trim, tidy and cool. The Ambassador had gone over to see the Americans, but wanted Rupert to lunch with him. A little breeze ruffled the rhododendrons in the garden. It was almost incredible that yesterday the country had nearly been at war, Claudia had died and Lambakis had been murdered.

'I don't suppose you'll want to go to the Marides funeral, will you?' Janet asked. 'Stephen said he'd look out for all of us if that was all right by you.'

'Anything he suggests. I have Claudia's to arrange.'

'I've suggested the undertaker comes here at three. If you don't want to see him I'll cope.'

'Right. Where's Elissa?'

'Up in her room. I've been trying to book her plane tickets but there's a terrible back-log. I haven't spoken to Cantrell yet. I thought I'd hold the high brass in reserve.'

He went up to the guest room and flew into her arms. The children looked up for a moment or two surprised, and then went on with the card game they were playing.

'Are you all right?' he asked anxiously.

'Yes. Are you? I'm so sorry about it all.'

'We'll survive. I'm glad you didn't go back with Marides.'

'It's silly, really. Just instinct, that's all. I feel something's still brewing and I don't want to be involved.'

'And you still don't know what it is?'

'No.' She looked at him straight in the eyes. 'Honestly I don't know what it is.'

'Well then, we'd better get you back to London as soon as we can. It doesn't look now as if it can be until tomorrow at least.'

Now that he had her in his arms, only letting her go with reluctance, the full urge of his loneliness took him. The emptiness of his heart, as it had been all these years, seemed now impossible to bear. He had forgotten for so long what it was like to be in love that now the old pleasurable ache simply overwhelmed him. She smiled at him as if she knew what he was feeling.

'Women are wonderful,' he said. 'You all suggest instant understanding when in fact you're calculating whether you were gypped over the vegetables.'

'Men aren't so bad at it either,' she retorted. 'How about you – now – at this time?'

'Oh God, don't bring the guilt back. You're the only person I know who doesn't make me feel guilty – so don't start now.'

'I really am sorry about Claudia. I mean, I'm sorry she had such a frustrated unhappy life. I'm sorry it didn't come right for her before she died. It doesn't seem fair.'

'It wasn't and it isn't for any of us.'

'You really are a cynic, aren't you?'

'Not about you.'

The sudden hard glint came back into her eyes and she made a restless movement of her hands. It was like a door slamming shut in the wind.

'That's just the other side of the coin. Sentimentality and cynicism are simply two halves of one whole. You learn that at school.'

The door was not only shut: it had iron spikes sticking out of it. Then he saw her looking at the children playing at the other end of the room. Something in her expression, a look he had once or twice been given by her himself, made him remember with a stab of pain that the children and their father were to Elissa what Claudia had been to him, a fundamental problem – something in the way, something they might never get around, something which could never be completely forgotten.

'I'm afraid I was a little hard on your Mrs Tarnham,' the Ambassador said to Rupert over lunch. 'Perhaps you would tactfully convey my regrets. I suppose she really can't be blamed if you bring her into the Embassy. It's scarcely her fault.'

It occurred to Rupert that this was probably as near to an apology as Harborough would ever get. He felt called on to explain.

'What was going on at the Marides' house looked ugly to me. We obviously had no idea Lambakis was going to be disposed of in a matter of hours. In the meantime the Security Police made a nasty mess of the son.'

'What have they done?'

'Knocked out two teeth, crushed his toes and electrified his genitals, though I understand that doesn't show. They're a pleasant lot, these Eastern Mediterranean Nazis.'

'I'm not clear how Lambakis got where he did nor specifically what he was after.'

'Well, power of course. He made a miscalculation, that's all. He banked on a short sharp war between Turkey and Greece which would enable him to grab what he wanted. Unfortunately Marides has the hard cash and keeps the present lot more or less where he wants them. If they don't exactly eat out of his hand, they do what he tells them, so to get where he wanted Lambakis had to neutralize him and his son. He didn't realize that Marides had thought out the possibilities more deeply than that.'

It seemed to Rupert that Harborough was pleased about something. This would normally have made him suspicious, but today he put it down to the general feeling of relaxation which enveloped everything now that the war was off. He gave the Ambassador a running account of what had happened since his departure. In turn he probed as best he could how things had gone in London. He did not particularly enjoy being treated to an hour-by-hour account of what took place in Whitehall, but he hoped that Harborough would mention Stevens and arrive without prompting at a discussion of his own future. But Harborough was riding his favourite hobby horse – the pressures on the higher echelons of the Civil Service and the growing impossibility of getting a quick decision on any normal matter of policy in a reasonable time. He expressed, as always on such occasions, the singularly unoriginal thought that this was paving the way for dictatorship in England. This, he concluded, was probably what the country needed.

At last Rupert could contain his impatience no longer. 'Did you manage to see Stevens?' he asked. 'And is there any news of a move for me?'

A glint of satisfaction came into Harborough's eyes. He had evidently been waiting for this. 'Yes, Rupert, I did.' He paused as if measuring his words. 'I'm afraid it isn't encouraging. Of course Stevens was as non-committal as ever, but it was rather the thumbs-down, I'm sorry to tell you. Frankly it doesn't look as though there *is* anything for you in the immediate future. You'll just have to soldier on here. Very disappointing, I know, but there it is.'

The Ambassador could scarcely keep the pleasure out of his voice nor the barely suppressed smile off his face. He had once admitted to Rupert that in his opinion the way to stay at the top of the ladder was to wait until your competitor had his hands on the rung below and then stamp hard on the knuckles. It was not what S. Bannister would have done. But this was the little man's moment of satisfaction – the vindication of all the Establishment ideas to which he was so enslaved and which had made him what he was. Rupert felt sick. He could scarcely bear to be in the presence of such meanness of spirit.

'It's a bad time for you, Rupert, I'm afraid. Claudia's sudden death and now this. I do sympathize. Perhaps you'd like to take some of your leave before it's due. I expect we could stretch a point if that would be of help. You're not strictly eligible, but I'm sure I can wangle it for you.'

'Very kind of you,' Rupert said. 'I might take a few days off and see Stevens myself.'

'Why don't you indeed? You won't get anywhere with him, but at least it would clear your mind and you could get it straight from the horse's mouth.'

'Yes,' Rupert said, feeling the life dying away in him. 'I might do as you suggest.'

XIV

SO MOURNIER had been right. As the day wore on he remembered, as clearly as if it had been five minutes ago, that scene on the Marides' beach, the look and even the intonation with which Mournier had said: 'When Harborough returns from London, I'm afraid he'll have some rather disappointing news for you – from Stevens. You're being dropped. You'll simply soldier on in the sort of post you're holding down now . . .' How could he possibly have known unless the truth was that the Service had been penetrated right at the top? Or was it simply that they had the appointments and records in their power? From Stevens they could easily have discovered that he was low in the promotion stakes. But could they honour the other side of the deal? '. . . in your case the consideration we offer is something of much greater value – an embassy of your own.' There was only one way of finding that out. Perhaps it was still a trap to test his loyalty – though why anyone should bother he did not know. Perhaps in any case it was now too late. He felt deeply depressed, tired and anxious, and now out of a hard unhappiness he began to give the deal some further thought. It was a strange sensation, even to be playing with the idea of doing a Tarnham.

By the evening he had all but worked himself dry. Harborough had been exacting; the Greek political situation had had to be analysed in the light of the war that wasn't, the murder of Lambakis and the changing power structure. He wrote, dictated, talked and tried to free himself of the numbness which he was now beginning to feel would be with him for life. Janet had succeeded in getting Elissa and the children bookings for London the following afternoon. Claudia's funeral was fixed for the day after. Beyond stretched a nothingness he did not care to think about. As dusk began to fall he sat alone in his office, smoking his pipe, his eyes on the darkening garden, his spirit brooding.

'Isn't there anything I can do?' Janet asked. By this time he had told her he was not expecting any letter from Stevens and the implications of this made her burn with an inner rage.

'No, Janet, we've done enough for the present.'

'I didn't really mean work. I hate seeing you so low.'

She had never risked talking intimately to him before. It was almost as if she felt older than him, as if he were a little boy she had to comfort.

'You're a very sweet girl, Janet, and I'm very grateful to have you. But I don't think there's anything you or anyone else can do for me just at present. Aren't you going to this party at the Czech Embassy?'

'I don't think so. I'm rather bored with helping Stephen do his job.'

'Is that what he asks you to do?'

The unspoken implication that Axley had asked her to spy on him showed as a question in his eyes and an answer in hers.

'Sort of.'

'I must have been giving the pair of you sleepless nights.'

'I'm fed up with it,' Janet said, 'and I'm fed up with him as well. He's like a schoolboy playing at cops and robbers.'

'It's the game he has to play, Janet – that we all of us have to play. If you weren't prepared for that sort of thing you shouldn't have joined government service.'

'Well, anyway I wasn't going to spy on you.'

'But you should, Janet.' He was surprising himself with this bland duplicity, considering what was then in his mind. 'After Philby which of us can ever be relied on again?'

'You can,' Janet said stoutly. 'I don't care what they suspect, you've got integrity. You'd never defect.'

'Wouldn't I? How do you know I'm not already a card-carrying Communist?'

'Good Lord!' She gave a short laugh. 'You're not, are you?'

'I wouldn't be too sure – but the point is how do you know? How does anyone know any more? The whole business of loyalty is in question these days.'

'I'm not so sure. Integrity's still integrity, isn't it?'

Shades of S. Bannister, he thought; she'll be telling me next that it's what you are that matters.

'My father's always saying, "It's the end of the Roman Empire",' she went on, 'only it's the Civil Service eating us up from the inside out. But people are still people.' She glanced at him with a little smile. 'You're all right.'

'Thank you, Janet.' She looked so young and ravishing in her mini-skirt, he felt his heart leap unexpectedly. 'It's nice having you around. You're a lovely girl.'

They studied each other briefly across the generation gap and knew that each understood the other on a basis of mutual liking, even love. It was the only solvent in human relationships which actually changed things for the better.

'Since we're talking to each other at last,' she said, perching on the edge of his desk, 'this may be a tactless moment to say it – but you will marry her, won't you?'

'I don't know, Janet. It depends on her. And the children don't seem to take to me much.'

'What sort of person was Tarnham?'

'He was much more intense than I was. I suppose he was a stronger man.'

'I doubt it.'

'Well, a firmer one with more drive and determination, if you like. The sort of man who would have become a Gordon of Khartoum in other times. Religious, I suppose.'

'It sounds as if he didn't have much sense of humour.'

'He had charm and a sort of aggressive thrust into life. People with senses of humour seem to stop themselves short. It's certainly a dangerous asset if you're at all ambitious.'

At that moment Elissa came into the room. Janet excused herself with the sort of ease, Rupert reflected, which poor Claudia had never in her life achieved. Claudia had always made things awkward; this girl floated in and out in a natural way without generating any artificial heat.

'I'll be in the library if you want me.'

'I can't think why I should at this hour,' Rupert said. 'Everyone else in the Embassy seems to have gone home. You'd better make up for the last few days, too, and get yourself some sleep.'

'I'll look in anyway before I go.'

When they were alone, he and Elissa held each other tenderly and kissed at length.

'I'm going to miss you,' she said.

'But not for long, I hope.'

'I don't know,' she said. 'I just don't know.'

After a short pause he said: 'I'm not being promoted – Harborough brought the glad news back from London. I might just as well retire and get some other job.'

She did not seem to be unduly surprised. He supposed this was another thing she had known all along.

'If I were to do that,' he went on, 'you would marry me, wouldn't you?'

'It's possible,' she said. 'I'd have to see how I felt at the time.'

On each occasion they met they seemed to have to fence with each other in that way.

'I suppose you knew I wasn't going to get an embassy,' he could not help saying.

She smiled with her eyes. 'On the contrary I thought you'd be bound to get one. I think you still will. This is only a temporary delay.'

'So you are aware of what it's all about?'

'No, I'm just making an informed guess.'

'You really *don't* know why they're interested in me?'

'I realize they are, as I told you, but I don't know why.'

He looked at her standing over by the french windows to the garden. She was strongly desirable to him – physically and in her being – as no other woman had been before. He knew that what he was going to say would hurt her or at least surprise her so he hesitated a moment or two longer.

'I knew Paul was going to defect.'

'No!' It was a deep cry, almost an animal sound.

'I knew that would be a shock to you after all this length of time.'

'You mean you had suspicions? You didn't definitely know?'

'He told me. I didn't believe him. I never thought, when it came to the point, that he'd go, but I knew his intentions.'

'He never told *me* – his wife. I was his wife.'

'I didn't enjoy the knowledge.'

'But why should he tell you and not me?'

'I'm not sure. Perhaps he didn't trust—' He paused, feeling for the words which would not hurt her too much. 'Perhaps he didn't trust himself with you. I fancy he thought I might go as well. Another Burgess and Maclean. I was never sure of his thinking. Only that he told me he was going to do it about a week before he went.'

'Why didn't you do anything about it?'

'I didn't believe him. Then when he did go, I rather naturally had an aversion to cutting my own throat.'

'And you kept that knowledge secret through all the investigations?'

'Absolutely. And obviously. Otherwise I wouldn't be here.'

'No wonder they're interested in you now.' Then it broke out of her again like a cry of pain: 'But what about me – me and the children? He just left us like all his old clothes.'

'I think he was tortured by what he knew he was doing to you.'

'Ha!' She gave a half-laugh, half-cry. 'Some torture – yet he did it. That's how valuable *we* were in his life.' She was crying now, silently, the tears simply starting out of her eyes and rolling down her cheeks. He took her in his arms but she scarcely responded.

'The bastard!' she said in a low voice. 'The rotten bastard!'

'You do really love him, don't you?' Rupert said, aware once again of the old familiar chill at the base of the spine, the old loser's tingle.

'Of course I love him!' she said with such an intensity of fury and in such a low controlled voice that Rupert dropped his arms and moved slightly away. 'I think I could kill him now.'

Janet came into the room. Elissa turned towards the garden so that her face was not visible. Rupert went back to his desk.

'I think I'll be off now,' Janet said, 'if you've nothing else. Everyone else has gone, except for the duty staff. H.E.'s at the Czech Embassy and so is Stephen. I think I'll have an early night as you suggest.'

Rupert nodded his approval, when the phone rang. Janet picked it up.

'Who? No, the Counsellor has no appointments so far as I know at this hour of the evening.' She cupped the phone. 'Is this something private?' she asked Rupert. 'He says his name is Jaroslav.'

'No. Never heard of him.'

'I'm sorry, Mr Jaroslav, the Counsellor can't receive you now. Would you care to make an appointment for another time?' She listened to the voice at the other end, not liking what she heard. 'All right, I'll ask.' Again she cupped the phone: 'He says he must see you tonight, that it's very urgent. He wants to talk to you now.'

Glancing at Elissa, Rupert took over the phone impatiently.

'Mr Jaroslav, you heard what my secretary said. I have no appointments at this time of night . . . who are you? *Who?* All right, wait a minute.' For a second or two he froze into complete stillness, covering the phone with his hand, and looking into the distance. He was aware of Janet's attention. He had to act with care, with very great care indeed and also with the utmost urgency. The adrenalin was pumping into his body. He began trembling like an athlete at the start of a race. He spoke quietly to Janet.

'Take Elissa out – that way through the Ambassador's office – up to her room. Stay with her and the children and under no circumstances whatever let her come down here unless I send for you.' He spoke into the phone. 'All right, I'll see you in a moment.'

Putting down the phone he went over to Elissa. Once again the training of a lifetime came to his aid, and he kept invisible the tremors which seemed to be wracking his body.

'I'm afraid I've got to see someone rather urgently,' he said. 'Would you go up to your room with Janet? I'll let you know when I'm free again.'

Without a word Elissa did as she was told and she and Janet left him alone. Rupert drew the curtains quickly and glanced at his desk to see it was clear. Then the door to the hall opened and in came the visitor. For a moment or so they looked at each other in total silence. Then Rupert went over to greet him.

'Hallo, Paul, welcome back.'

'Hallo, Rupert.'

To Rupert's eyes he seemed unchanged from three years ago. There was still the same determined set to the head, the same innate superiority of the committed, the arrogance of the man who knows.

'I must say you have a nerve. You haven't forgotten this is technically British soil you're on?'

'I'm not in the danger you think I am. I'm now a Czech citizen with a valid passport and visa for Greece. Your ambassador is now drinking sherry with ours. However, I don't have much time. Nor do you.'

'Why have you come here at all?'

'To get Elissa and the children.'

'And me?'

'Since you've come straight to the point – yes.'

There was a pause while he simply looked at Paul Tarnham through three years of a wrecked career. It was a long cool look.

'The answer is no.'

'I don't understand. You can't prevent my wife and children joining me if they want to—'

'That's the key question, isn't it? If they want to. I can certainly prevent them and you from leaving the British Embassy – the more so in view of your background and the attempt you're making to suborn me. You were many years in the Foreign Service, Paul – you know the form as well as I do.'

'Very well, let's not argue about details. You're being offered a chance – if you don't choose to accept it that's up to you. Now I'd like to see Elissa and the children.'

'Would you indeed?'

'I have a car outside. All the necessary arrangements are made. If any questions are asked here about her abrupt departure, you'll simply say she decided to go back to the Marides.'

'I can't believe it, Paul,' he said with an easy authority. 'Are you telling *me* what to do? You've got the nerve to march in here and give orders to me!' He laughed shortly. 'You must be very sure of yourself indeed.'

'I am. We are, if you prefer it. If I wasn't one hundred per cent certain of the way we work, do you think I'd put my head in the lion's den? Now, where is she? Or do I go and find her myself?'

'You make one move from this room, Paul, and I'll have you under arrest.' He put his hand on the phone. 'And you know I'm not bluffing. It's probably my duty to do that anyway.'

'It may be but you won't.'

'Won't I?'

'Because if you did the facts of my departure and your prior knowledge of them will be placed, fully documented, where they can do you the most damage. You must have known we could always do that. But you've never pushed things to the limit – that's why we want you to work for us, Rupert, as Mournier suggested on Sunday.'

'I don't have your ideological disease.'

'You used to be more to the left than I was.'

'Never – and I'm not now.'

'Well, that part of the past doesn't matter,' Tarnham said impatiently. 'What does matter is now.'

'How do you come to be here at all? They must certainly trust you a lot.'

'Now come on, Rupert,' Tarnham said. 'I'm not here for a chat.'

'That's right, Paul, and now that I come to think of it neither am I. However, as you have put your head in the lion's den – like it or not – you'll damn well take the consequences.'

XV

LOOKING back on it afterwards Rupert saw the progression of this extraordinary meeting almost as if it were taking place in a court of law. The judge and the jury were both invisible, yet their presence was felt. It was only afterwards that he defined it to himself in this way. At the time, although he felt himself on safe ground both physically in that he was Her Britannic Majesty's Counsellor in Her Britannic Majesty's Embassy in Athens, and in spirit since he still had his integrity, nevertheless the danger in which he stood tensed him to breaking point. So much was at stake. The easy line, which his duty dictated, was simply to hold Tarnham in the Embassy until the Ambassador returned.

Had he done that the dialogue would then have come abruptly to an end. A Press and Parliamentary furore would have blown up again, and the Tarnham affair would have had its last national and international airing. But this was not the way it went.

As he studied Paul Tarnham across his desk in the quietness of his room, he realized that the crucible in which the elements were now being tested was a personal one. In the end you had nothing but yourself. It was his heart, his spirit – in essence his life – which was now in front of the court.

'You're in love with Elissa,' Paul said, 'and you want to marry her.'

'Yes.'

'Why have you prevented her from going back to the Marides' house?'

'I haven't. She's afraid. She asked to stay on here herself.'

'I don't believe you. You're holding her here for personal and squalid reasons of your own.'

'She's here of her own free will.'

He had not realized how powerful was the malignancy in Paul. Or was this only from the conventional, Western point of view?

'I'll make you a deal.'

'I doubt it. Mournier tried and failed.'

'This is a better one,' Paul said. 'I'll offer you everything Mournier did on Sunday, plus Elissa.'

The cynicism was so blatant it took his breath away. He paused a long time before answering. His heart ached at the pity of it. The pity and the grief. Well – there it was.

'I don't think I heard you correctly.'

'Now come on, Rupert, forget your cosy bourgeois ideas for a moment. You're not a religious man. Your immortal soul is scarcely endangered. I'm simply making you an offer which will never again come your way. Say yes and I'll leave now as quietly as I came. Elissa will never know I've been here. No one will know. Let her go back tomorrow. I'll take the pressure off her. In fact if she tries to come to Russia now she'll find it impossible. From then on it's up to you. If you're not man enough to make her marry you then

– well, that's it. You couldn't be given more of a following wind.'

'You sod!' he said in a low voice. 'You rotten sod!'

He had nothing to match the sneer and contempt which Tarnham allowed to show briefly in his eyes. Tarnham went on calmly, almost lightly:

'This isn't a Victorian melodrama, Rupert. Why don't you bring yourself up to date with the world as it is today?'

'I don't understand you. Perhaps I never will.'

'You certainly made one staggering miscalculation – not that things would have been much different for you if you hadn't.'

'She's your wife. She loves you. Doesn't that mean anything to you?'

'Of course.' The cold eyes projected an implacability Rupert could not recall ever having seen before. 'What an infantile question! She's my wife and I have two children by her. But you were proposing to steal her. I'm giving her to you instead. Isn't that a more civilized way of going about a rather tricky problem than the hypocrisy it usually generates?'

'I was not going to steal her – or anything else. If she decided to divorce you and marry me that would be of her own free will. *Her* free will and no one else's.'

'Oh yes, free will! I'd forgotten the old capitalist jargon. Two cheers for free will.'

'Suppose I tell her of the offer you've just made to me?'

'You won't. If you tell her later on she'll never forgive you for letting me come within a few feet of her without saying I was here. If you bring her in now, while I'm here, I shall simply deny it – and you'll certainly lose her. You know and I know, Rupert, that once she sets eyes on me again your chances are nil. Not because your sexual prowess is in any way inferior to mine, but because of one simple fact, which you've just pointed out – she loves me.'

The dagger was in. Now he had to avoid bleeding to death . . .

'There's a third course open to me,' Rupert said, 'and

that is simply to arrest you here and now pending investigation of your defection three years ago.'

'You must be joking, dear boy. This operation was very carefully planned and – except for the unfortunate Mr Lambakis – has worked entirely as intended. You don't really think I'd be fool enough to enter a British embassy without having taken every necessary precaution, do you? You arrest me and your best three agents in Russia are shot out of hand tomorrow. I'm sorry to bring in the thriller element, but we all know the form.'

'I think you're bluffing.'

'Think what you like. It doesn't worry me and it doesn't alter the facts.'

Elissa had had a moment of panic when she and Janet had gone back to her room. The children were not there. She opened the door and called 'Mark! Lucy!' without bothering to look. When there was no reply a sudden dread gripped her stomach – the 4 AM nightmare shudders – followed by an icy calm as her brain raced around the possibilities. The windows to the balcony were open and their toys scattered on the floor.

She walked to the balcony and looked down on the darkening garden. They could not have climbed down the wistaria and, although it was only on the first floor, it was too far to jump. Then she saw something at the end of the balcony which had certainly not been there before – a ladder up against the balustrade. There were pots of paint and a pail stacked in the corner, so no doubt they were going to start painting in the morning, and indeed she vaguely remembered being told about it.

She and Janet went quickly across to the ladder. Mark and Lucy were chasing each other on the lawn, watched by two men, dressed in overalls. She called down to the children and they stopped for a moment to say:

'We dared each other to climb down the ladder and these men gave us sweets.'

'Kala Meerasis,' she called to the men. One of them looked familiar but it was too dark to see their features. The larger man replied in friendly Greek which Elissa did not understand, and which Janet said was an invitation to climb down the ladder themselves.

'No, we'll come down the normal way,' she answered and moved swiftly back to the bedroom, followed by Janet.

'I'll go and get them,' Janet offered, but Elissa was off down the main staircase and out into the garden, almost at the run.

'That was very naughty of you,' she said to the children. 'You might have fallen and broken your necks.'

'Guess who's here,' Mark said, pointing to one of the men.

Elissa turned and found herself looking at Jean-Pierre Mournier, dressed somewhat improbably as a workman. The other man was of the gorilla type.

'What are you doing here?' she asked.

'Didn't you know I was in the contracting business?' he answered with a smile. 'You thought I was a diplomat, didn't you? But I'm really a contractor – one of the biggest in Athens.'

'Carrying about your own ladders and pots of paint?'

'Of course,' he replied lightly and equally mockingly. 'I take a personal interest in every job. Especially one as important as painting the British Embassy. Mark and Lucy were even more surprised than you were.'

'Who's your friend?' she asked.

'Oh, he's very talented. He contracts too, at least I think he does. He's also extremely handy with other things. Nikos, show Mrs Tarnham your trick.'

Almost instantaneously Nikos had acquired from an inner pocket a small poisonous-looking automatic. This was only visible to Elissa and Janet, who now began to move towards the french windows of the Counsellor's room.

'No, no, no!' Mournier said softly. 'That would be a very silly mistake. Just stay here with us, Miss Mortimer, while the children finish their game. Then no one will come to any harm. I don't suppose Mr Eynsham's visitor will keep him for very long.'

Behind the curtains which hid Rupert and Paul Tarnham from the garden there was a mounting urgency which derived, as indeed did the fight itself, from the invisible pressures of time. Rupert looked at his watch and realized that at any moment Harborough could return from his party at the Czech Embassy. Janet might be unable to keep control of Elissa and the children, if indeed she had them under control at all. Any other of the Embassy staff might return unexpectedly – or the duty officer might quite legitimately come in to see him, in which case Tarnham would be recognized and that would be that. He discounted the doorkeeper who had let in Mr Jaroslav. Except for the doorkeeper no one other than Rupert knew the identity of his visitor.

As if gauging his thinking Tarnham said:

'I told you – all this has been very carefully planned. It should have taken place at the Marides', but Sunday's accident and the Lambakis incident forced me to come here. However, Marides' yacht is arriving later tonight – should you wonder how I'm going to leave Fascist Greece without attracting attention, and of course if you don't avail yourself of our offer, Elissa and the children will be travelling in the same way.'

'I wonder.'

'Don't, Rupert. You're too intelligent to waste time.'

'I can't stomach your utter cynicism. To get me to work for you you're even prepared to barter your wife and family. It's monstrous – filthy – disgusting.'

The same hard calm smile broke the force of this outburst. After a pause Tarnham said:

'But you want her. You're in love with her.'

'Leave my feelings out of it. It's what you're doing that's loveless – I'd never have thought you capable of it.'

Tarnham laughed. 'Stop acting up a ladies' magazine

story of the thirties,' he said. 'This is the 1968 currency after all and there's no further devaluation possible. All I'm doing is giving you a chance to get the one thing I know you want – Elissa. She hasn't seen me for three years. She might conceivably settle for you – though God alone knows why. However, as you so blithely observed a short time ago, she still has her own free will. If she decides she really doesn't want you, she can still do one of two things – go back to England and pig it in Fulham as the brave little woman she is or make the break and join me in Russia. Think out the possibilities a little further, Rupert. Suppose she decides to take you on, and after living with you for a while it doesn't work out. She was still married to me for eight years or so – I'm still the father of her children. She can't be deprived of that. She has only to say the word, drop you like the flat pancake you seem to be – if I may say so – and join me as I've been urging her to do since I left. There – have I spelt it out enough for you in words of one syllable?'

'Let's keep Elissa out of it for a moment.' He still had a knife up his sleeve, and he used it now: 'Don't your children mean anything to you at all?'

He was watching Tarnham acutely and thought he detected a flicker of truth. There was a momentary pause.

'I'll level with you, Rupert, on that one. I do very much miss them indeed.'

'Yet you throw them overboard too.'

'We don't live by bread alone, as your man Christ pointed out.'

'Exactly. You opted for the bread.'

'Not at all. I did it – as well you know – for the most powerful motive in the world: ideological reasons. *You* may not understand, Rupert, but I now live among people who do. I'll be frank with you. I had hoped Elissa would forget politics, patriotism and all the other isms and come to me before now, with Mark and Lucy.'

'Why didn't you tell her you were going to defect? You must have known how much that would hurt her.'

For a moment Tarnham looked genuinely astonished.

'Good God Almighty, Rupert, hasn't that reason occurred to you even now?'

'No.'

'She was employed by MI6 of course. I should have thought that was obvious to a child of four.'

'And you knew that she was?'

'Of course I knew,' Tarnham said impatiently. 'I put them on to it. How else do you think she's here now? A false passport and Foreign Office assistance. Not even the British Government hands out that sort of thing for nothing. She was recruited when you first fell in love with her – to keep an eye on you. It was one of my better red herrings. Just as the heat was beginning to turn on me. However, don't worry about that now. I don't suppose they value her reports too highly. She's been nobbled, hasn't she, by us? And she's always missing the boat, isn't she? Like tonight.'

'What do you mean?'

'Like never knowing I was here.'

They exchanged a long concentrated look.

'You're assuming I'm going to say yes,' Rupert said quietly.

'Naturally. It's the only logical thing you can do.'

Out in the garden the one free element left to Elissa at that moment was the children. She and Janet were held under threat by Mournier and his gorilla. The children, chasing each other in a seemingly endless game of tig, were the only manoeuvrable pawns at that stage of the game.

'It's getting cold, children!' she called out, loudly enough, she hoped, for Rupert to hear. 'Time for bed.'

'They're happy,' Mournier said softly. 'Let them stay in the garden.'

'Why?'

'Just because. I won't keep you long.'

'What happens then?'

'You either go back to your room as if nothing whatever had happened or you all come with me.'

'Where to?'

'Out to your host, Panayotis Marides, of course. Where else?'

'What does the decision depend on?'

'Ah, now that is a difficult one to answer in a single sentence. Let's just say on forces beyond your control.'

Dusk had now turned into night. The children ended their game and came and stood by their mother. Elissa could scarcely suppress the fear generated by the gorilla's gun and, from the look on her face, this fear also controlled Janet. She hoped it would not spill over on to the children. But fear like sex communicates instantly.

'Why are you shivering, Mummy?' Lucy asked.

'Because it's very chilly – and late. It's time for bed. Come along now – we'll go upstairs.'

'Don't go yet,' Jean-Pierre Mournier said quietly but firmly. The gorilla performed his little trick so that both Elissa and Janet knew he had the gun in his hand. At that moment something suddenly fused in Janet, and all the old generals and admirals in her blood sprang into life.

'Keep the children beside you,' she said to Elissa. 'I'll go and get Mr Eynsham.'

Then, inwardly quaking with fear, she began to walk towards the french windows with the drawn curtains and the light behind.

'Come back here, Miss Mortimer,' Mournier said. She paid no attention, said nothing and went on. Then things happened at great speed. The gun cracked, the children screamed and Janet staggered, the bullet having nicked her thigh.

'No, no!' Mournier said furiously to the gorilla. 'With the hands!'

He leapt after Janet, clapped a hand over her mouth and held her.

'It's all right, children,' Elissa said, huddling them on either side of her with an arm around their shoulders. She began to move towards Rupert's room.

'Stay where you are,' Mournier said, blocking the way.

'Go and fetch Uncle Rupert,' Elissa said urgently to Mark, who sped away to the french windows before Mournier could catch him. Then she and Lucy followed. Mournier knocked the child out of the way and held on to Elissa. Lucy began whimpering. With a surprising turn of speed Elissa brought her knee up hard into Mournier's groin and then, snatching up Lucy, ran to the french windows and thrust her way in through the curtains.

XVI

ON SEEING Paul she froze rigid. In fact there was a moment of complete stillness, like a stopped frame in an action film, the figures spaced about the room, each paralysed by surprise, each in a somehow characteristic attitude. In the distance an alarm bell was ringing and Rupert had the phone in his hand.

'Send the guard out on the terrace. No one is to enter or leave the Embassy. Let me know what you find as soon as you can.'

He put down the phone.

'Janet's been shot.' Elissa jerked her head towards the garden, and then turned and went out, followed by Rupert. There was no sign of Mournier or the gorilla. Janet was lying on the terrace trying to nurse her leg. Rupert picked her up and carried her into the room. She was bleeding from the fleshy part of the thigh but the wound was no more than a superficial graze.

'Shut the window. The doorkeeper has a first-aid box in the hall. Mark, go and get it from him now.'

The boy sped away, glad of something to do. Lucy had

stopped crying and was looking fascinated at the blood from Janet's thigh and then in equal fascination at her father. The duty officer came running in.

'They've gone,' he said and then, seeing Janet: 'I'd better get Dr Vakelopoulos.'

'I'm all right,' Janet said. 'It's only a graze.'

The duty officer left and Mark returned with the first-aid box. Elissa and Rupert quickly bandaged the wound. While this was going on Tarnham made no effort to help, simply standing with his hands on the back of a chair, watching and waiting. Rupert poured some brandy from a flask he kept in one of his drawers and then they put Janet on a chaise longue by the window. The shock had made her very pale and Rupert sat beside her holding her hand.

In the meanwhile neither Elissa nor the children had approached their father. They simply stood there looking at him.

'You've certainly come back with your old panache,' Elissa said, staring at him, her emotions seething in her eyes.

The duty officer came back into the room.

'Dr Vakelopoulos is on his way. Shall I send for the police?'

Rupert hesitated a moment, looking first at Janet, trying to weigh up the different factors while there was still time.

'No – not for the moment. If the garden's clear you'd better search the building as well and report anything you find. Keep it to ourselves for the present.'

'That was wise at any rate,' Tarnham said after the duty officer had left. 'I don't think the Greek police will be of much help to you at a time like this.'

'I don't think it matters very much what you think,' Rupert said. 'You'll have all the answering to do later.'

'Are you implying that you're going to hold me here by force?'

'Yes.'

'You must be crazy. Have you forgotten what I just told you?'

'No. I don't necessarily believe everything you tell me, however.' A silence fell. Elissa and Paul were staring at each other but not moving. Rupert went on: 'Who were your friends in the garden?' The deep anger he felt was beginning to show in a curtness of tone. The fight was now on – the fight for Elissa, the fight for his life.

'Mournier was one of them,' Elissa said. 'The other was a real charmer, a sort of ape man. A thug with a gun.'

'Ah, the recruiter and his mate,' Rupert said. 'You brought them along too. Anyone else?'

'The Embassy is surrounded, if you want to know.'

Rupert smiled grimly. The verbal fencing might give them both time to adjust to the extraordinary emotional pressures in the room. It in no way altered the realities of the fight he had taken on.

'As if that mattered,' he said, 'or are you prepared to provoke a first-class international diplomatic incident?'

'Are *you*, Rupert?'

'Well, I don't see where the provocation is *this* end, but we won't lapse into semantics. Are your friends intending to invade the Embassy by force in order to extricate you? The drawbridge is up, you know, the boiling lead ready over the portcullis.'

'I don't think that will be necessary, Rupert. I'm sure we're going to agree on the best thing to do.' Then he turned his attention to Elissa: 'No greeting for me, Elissa? Hallo, Mark. Hallo, Lucy.'

They stared at each other, curiously rapt.

The children remained paralysed, both of them pale with shock.

'I came to get you,' Tarnham went on with a bland urbanity Rupert could not but admire in spite of himself. 'That is, of course, if you want to come.'

'He did nothing of the sort,' Rupert said quietly. 'He came to suborn me and offered you as part of the bargain, Elissa.'

'Believe that and you'll believe anything. And you were never that credulous, were you?'

'I think I am now,' Elissa said. She spoke as quietly as Rupert but with a suspicious catch in the voice. She and the two children still did not move. Eventually Paul stepped over towards her.

'Don't touch me!' she said sharply. 'I couldn't bear it if you touched me!'

'Come, come, Elissa' – he continued to approach her – 'that's a little hysterical, isn't it?'

Rupert placed himself so that there would have to be a direct confrontation for Paul to reach her. He was now coldly furious.

'Do as Elissa says. You are not in Russia now.'

'Brave words, Rupert, but whom do you think you are fooling? Who's impressed?' But he stopped nevertheless. 'What about the children? Aren't you going to say hallo to your father?'

Mark, followed by Lucy, came over and both rather woodenly allowed themselves to be hugged. Little was said and Rupert was astonished to see Paul's eyes fill with tears. The oppressive feeling in the room steadily mounted. It occurred to Rupert, in passing, that there was a Prussian quality in Paul which accounted both for his strength and for the ruthlessly suppressed emotionalism which filled the room. He glanced at Janet. She had her eyes fixed on Paul but was conscious of his own glance and gave him a flicker of encouragement, love, strength or whatever it was. In the heightened speed at which his brain and his heart were working it flashed through him with total inconsequence that he loved the girl. But this was a crisis-fired emotion, a sort of battleground love. From Janet he received a communication of courage by which the destiny can change. In that one look, though it went in a flash, they knew each other inside out. To Rupert it was an exchange of energy more real than the building in which they stood. Without putting it into words Rupert was aware, instantly and timelessly, of touching part of the invisible structure of the universe. Afterwards no doubt a slower process of thought would analyse and reject the experience and the idea behind it as fanciful nonsense. But ideas run the world, and at that moment of split-second awareness Rupert knew he had never been more alive in his life.

Now it was Elissa's turn. She too was looking at him, but this was a questioning, cooler look.

'Was that true, Paul? – what Rupert has just said, about trying to get him into the net?'

'That part of it, yes. He virtually has no alternative now. But you know that.'

'And was I included in the deal?'

'Of course not. You know that's absurd.'

She looked at him, cold as a stone. 'Liar!'

He did not immediately react. There were no tears now in his eyes. The snake-like expression had returned, and with it that veiled contemptuous smile.

'You can never prove it though.'

'I don't need proof. I know it.'

'Bully for you.'

Now Elissa was the prosecutor. 'So you don't really care whether we join you in Russia or not. All those letters, entreaties – all these last three years – it's all nonsense, isn't it? We've always come second to your sacred political ideas, haven't we – even before you went, when I thought we were an ordinary, reasonably happy family. We just weren't in the scene, were we?'

'An ordinary, reasonably happy family – is that the picture you had?'

'But instead it was Comrade Clever, wasn't it? All the time the only thing that mattered to you was drab, dreary, crashingly boring Communism. That first and us a million miles afterwards. Thank you, Paul, thank you for nine years of that. And above all, thank you for the last three years. Those have really made it for me.'

The chess analogy came vividly to Rupert's mind as he watched the progress of this part of the in-fighting. The Red King was in check with his two pawns on either side of him. Elissa, the White Queen, had him covered by himself, perhaps as a Bishop and by Janet, on the sofa, as a

Castle. Mate in how many moves? In the meantime the Red King moved out of check behind his pawns.

'A fine speech,' Paul said. 'However, we're all a little pressed for time. I need a decision.'

'I'll give you one right away,' Elissa cut in as if every word had a razor edge. 'Not in a million years would I join you now. Nor will the children.'

There was a significant pause. Paul had his hands on the shoulders of his children to either side of him. Both had remained as white as paper.

'You will, you know,' Paul said calmly, 'and you know it.' Watching them both intently, Rupert could almost see her icy will melting in the corrosiveness of the stare.

'Come here, children.' Elissa said. For a moment neither moved. 'Well?' she said. Still neither of them moved, nor did anyone else in the room. Then Paul lifted his hands off their shoulders. The tears were back in his eyes. A total silence held them all.

'Well?' Elissa said once again. Lucy ran across the room and buried her face in her mother's skirt. Mark remained rigid and as if transfixed, his father's hand still poised over his shoulder like a priest giving a benediction. Elissa questioned her son with her eyes.

'I'm ... I'm staying with Father,' the boy said in a whisper. 'Sorry ...'

Paul's hand came down once more on the shoulder. It was certainly not checkmate.

'No one's staying with anyone,' Rupert said, 'except you, Paul, and that is here. You're under arrest, Czech passport, visa and all. I don't think there's much your friends outside can do about it – if indeed they are there at all. In any case it's a risk I've decided to take.'

'Sorry, Rupert,' Paul said, producing a small automatic from his pocket, 'but it isn't quite as easy as that.' He had his left hand on the boy's shoulder and his right, holding the gun unseen by Mark, a few inches behind the boy's head. Elissa stifled a cry and in turn kept Lucy's head buried in her skirt. 'I said we were pressed for time. Since you won't accept the offer I've made you I simply withdraw and leave you to face your own brand of music, and what you know will be coming your way. Now pick up the phone and arrange for the doorkeeper to let us both walk out of the front door. Go on.'

No one moved. Rupert looked across at Elissa and raised his eyebrows in question.

'I'm afraid he might,' she said softly.

The mean little smile was back on Paul's lips. 'You can be sure he will,' Paul said.

Still no one moved. It occurred to Rupert that if no one did anything at all then Paul would be forced sooner or later to some action himself. The point was what would he do? If he was as mad as he seemed then he was fully likely to regard any or all of them, including his own son, as expendable.

'You know you can't really get away with this, Paul,' Rupert said. 'For God's sake don't fool around in that way!'

'Oh, but I can and I shall. Hurry up with that phone. Go on.' The Prussian was visible again. The boy still had no idea that his father was holding a gun a few inches behind his head.

'Paul, you do realize, don't you, that the duty officer is coming back through that door at any moment? You can't get away with it.'

'You'd be surprised. You may think I'm mad. I can assure you I'm not. And I don't intend to be crucified. We made you an offer which you might well have accepted, and things would then have come right for you in a miraculous way. But that offer had to remain a secret. That's why we had to use force. We failed in that and your secretary unfortunately got in the way. So it's no longer a secret and the deal is off. But don't you yet understand? Our ability to make things happen at much higher levels than yourself remains. It's there whether you work for us or not, whether you try and crucify me or not. It isn't touched by any of this.'

'I don't believe you.'

'It doesn't matter whether you do or not. It's a fact. Now pick up that phone and do as I say.'

There was a second or two of complete silence. Now Rupert felt the actual physical presence of those great nameless forces which change the life. Be still and know that I am God. Be still. Even the breathing seemed scarcely to be there. He stared at Elissa, imploring her with his eyes. A sad, smoky look drifted into her face and at that point he knew he had lost. He realized that what Paul had said earlier on was abysmally true: 'You know and I know, Rupert, that once she sets eyes on me again your chances are nil. Not because your sexual prowess is in any way inferior to mine, but because of one simple fact – she loves me.' None of the other reasons, none of the pressing ulterior motives which had severally drawn them together in this room, had any validity now. The simple significance which he now saw shining out of her like a light was that do what he might she was bound to Paul by an emotion she could not resist, of a power and a depth to which he could not attain.

As if confirming his thought, she turned to him, almost imperceptibly shaking her head.

'I'm so sorry, Rupert,' she said softly and then paused, feeling for the words: 'But you understand. I know you understand. So – now – will you please let us all go?'

Although he had been aware instinctively of what she was going to say, the shock of hearing her actually bring out the words almost paralysed his will. He searched in her eyes for a ray of hope, for some more explicit reason for the volte-face he knew he would have to accept, but it was like looking into a deep pool from high up on a cliff. He was baffled and his heart ached.

'You can't ask him for that,' Janet said from the sofa. 'You can't.'

'All of you – just go like that?'

'Please, Rupert. Paul, put that thing away.'

Tarnham slipped the gun back in his pocket and then gave Rupert a smile. 'See?'

'You know what they'll do to him if he lets you go,' Janet said, but again no one paid any attention. 'He'll be the one to be crucified.'

'Please, Rupert... please!'

The duty officer came in from the hall.

'I've searched the building and it's clear. Shall I call the police about the incident on the terrace?'

'No,' Rupert said. 'We don't want the Greek police in on this.'

'I'll bring in Dr Vakelopoulos when he arrives.' He looked questioningly at Paul.

It was obvious that the duty officer had no idea of Mr Jaroslav's real identity and did not connect him with the incidents in the garden. But there was now no time left. At any moment Harborough or Axley or any of the others could walk in. Perhaps Janet would stand by him. Perhaps if she kept her mouth shut, something could be saved from the wreckage.

'All right, that's all for the moment. I'll show Mr Jaroslav out myself.'

'Very good, sir.' The duty officer left.

Rupert turned to Elissa. They were now as strangers to each other.

'If you're going out to the Marides' tonight, you'll be wanting to pack. Why don't you do that now?'

They all left the room together. He could not bear to look at her. Elissa and the children went upstairs. Out in the hall Rupert signed to the doorkeeper, who unlocked the front door.

'Thank you, Rupert,' Paul said out of earshot of the doorkeeper. 'I'm sorry you couldn't see things our way. We'd have looked after you well.'

Rupert said nothing. He watched Paul walk down the short Embassy drive to a car parked on the other side of the street. Then, turning back into the Embassy, he made his way slowly along to his room.

XVII

AS SOON as she could get to her feet Janet, scarcely able to walk, hobbled upstairs to have it out with Elissa. She was in a blazing fury.

'You can't go! You can't do this to him! It'll kill him!'

'Nonsense. You know why I'm going. Wait till you have children of your own.'

'It's still not too late. Anyway your filthy husband only wanted to get out and save his own skin. He doesn't want you or your children.'

'He's still my husband. I know him better than you do. I know what he would have done. Also I happen to be living *my* life – not yours or anyone else's.'

'Rupert loves you. He's a good man.'

'I should take this from you!' Elissa snapped. 'If he's so marvellous, marry him yourself.'

'Maybe I would if he asked me. That's not the point.'

'The point is that we're now packed and we're going.'

'You've wrecked his life. You and that shoddy little traitor you married.'

'Who are you – God's daughter? What the hell is it to do with you?'

'And I thought you were so wonderful. One of the most super women I've ever met.'

She was half-crying with rage. Lucy was whimpering miserably by the bed. Mark watched stonily silent.

'Yes, well now you know the other side of the coin. It's no good getting angry with me. We all do what we have to do.'

'Don't you believe in anything any more?'

'Yes I do,' Elissa said with a hard precision. 'In survival.'

'And you call what you're doing – that?'

Elissa snapped shut the last suitcase and straightened up. 'Look, Janet, you're a nice, well-brought-up English girl. Just as super as you thought I was. But how old are you? Twenty – twenty-one? You don't know what it's about. You really don't. Any jam you get into and Nanny or Mummy or Daddy are there to get you out of it. Well, life isn't like that any more – and there's nothing you can do about other people either. You can't change them and they can't change you. Now – do you think someone could help us down with these bags?'

The duty officer brought in Dr Vakelopoulos, a man of understanding with a large embassy practice. One look between him and Rupert was enough to establish the urgency and secrecy of the visit.

'We had thieves who broke into the Embassy grounds,' Rupert said, 'and unfortunately my secretary was shot in the leg.'

'You've reported this to the police?'

'No. There are circumstances which make this undesirable.'

'I understand.'

The duty officer took him away to examine Janet. The doorkeeper informed him that the Marides' car was at the door for Mrs Mathews.

'You might help her down with her bags then.'

'That's done, sir. They're in the hall waiting. Is it all right to let them go?'

'Yes,' Rupert said, turning away so that his face was not visible to the doorkeeper. 'Let them go. Let me know when they've gone.'

His instinct was to rush out after him, to cling to Elissa, to hold her tight. 'Don't go! Don't go!' his heart cried out in an agony of loneliness. But he made no move except to draw back the curtains and gaze at the dark garden as he had done so many times before. The pain he felt was almost unbearable and yet ... and yet, now that it was over, his mind began to grope its way back into control. The mind was what mattered now. 'Life is a cabaret, old chum, come to the cabaret', as the song had it. Well, one cabaret was over but his life went on. Or perhaps it was simply time to move down the street and sample another one. The mind, his somewhat underrated mind, could lift itself above the wreckage, the bleak hopelessness of it all, and bring back not only some sort of order into his life but also the comedy of the situation in which he had been left.

'Mrs Mathews and her children have gone,' the door-keeper reported, and Rupert thanked him for the information. Not even a whimper, let alone a bang. Dr Vakelopoulos looked in to say that he was taking Janet along to his clinic to treat her wound and put in some stitches, but that there was no danger to her at all and that she had been excessively lucky – the bullet had missed an important artery ... but Rupert politely cut him short with a smile and sent him on his way. This was too rare and valuable a moment to waste on explanatory details.

Once again he was alone, completely and utterly alone as at birth or at death. The trees in the garden moved slightly in the night wind which often sprang up at this time as if to blow away the sweaty heat of the day. It was a lovely garden and he thought in passing of Claudia and of the fact that gardens were one of the few things she had loved in her wracked, inhibited life. Well, she was well out of it now. She could never have endured the hullaballoo which was about to begin. He would survive, however – there was now nothing else which could happen to him.

Suddenly he found himself laughing outright. The scene which he knew would soon take place with Harborough, and perhaps with Axley in attendance, was what a playwright would call a *scène-à-faire*, an oligatory and essential part of the play. Fear now had vanished. He was going to enjoy it immensely – because what, after all, could they possibly do to him now?

He visualized it all as it would soon be enacted. It would be triggered off by the duty officer's report of the shooting incident in the garden.

'It was particularly unfortunate timing,' he heard himself saying to the Ambassador, 'because Paul Tarnham and I were just getting to grips with the deal he was offering me.' This would be the first mention of Tarnham he would make, and he had no intention of losing control of the scene from then on. In prospect he could already enjoy their appalled astonishment that Tarnham had come and gone while they were at the Czech Embassy. He would then continue with a brief description of the post-Philby certainty that the Service had been penetrated at the very highest levels. 'So you see, Ambassador, I'll put you in a very full report of these last few days in Greece, which you will have to submit with your own considered comments to the dear old Foreign Office, and then we shall wait and see. I may, of course, be instantly suspended. There is bound to be an inquiry. But as the Press are not on to this, I feel sure that secrecy is going to win the day for all of us. And who knows – I may get my own embassy yet! Why not Czechoslovakia? Perhaps you could suggest it.'

He was still laughing to himself when Jean-Pierre Mournier came quietly along the terrace, opened the french windows and shot him three times through the heart.

A SELECTION OF POPULAR READING IN PAN

FICTION

William Mitford
☐ LOVELY SHE GOES! 30p (6/–)
Agatha Christie
☐ THE ADVENTURE OF THE CHRISTMAS PUDDING 25p (5/–)
☐ THEY DO IT WITH MIRRORS 25p (5/–)
Ian Fleming
☐ ON HER MAJESTY'S SECRET SERVICE 20p (4/–)
A new James Bond novel by Robert Markham
☐ COLONEL SUN 25p (5/–)
John le Carré
☐ THE SPY WHO CAME IN FROM THE COLD 25p (5/–)
☐ THE LOOKING-GLASS WAR 25p (5/–)
☐ A SMALL TOWN IN GERMANY 30p (6/–)
Robert Miall
☐ UFO 25p (5/–)
☐ UFO Vol II 25p (5/–)
Frederick E. Smith
☐ WATERLOO (illus.) 25p (5/–)
Juliette Benzoni
☐ CATHERINE AND A TIME FOR LOVE 35p (7/–)
George MacDonald Fraser
☐ FLASHMAN 30p (6/–)
Sergeanne Golon
☐ THE TEMPTATION OF ANGELIQUE I: The Jesuit Trap 30p (6/–)
☐ THE TEMPTATION OF ANGELIQUE II: Goldbeard's Downfall 30p (6/–)
☐ THE COUNTESS ANGELIQUE 1 25p (5/–)
☐ ANGELIQUE 1: The Marquise of the Angels 40p (8/–)
☐ ANGELIQUE IN REVOLT 30p (6/–)
☐ ANGELIQUE AND THE SULTAN 30p (6/–)
☐ ANGELIQUE AND THE KING 30p (6/–)
Arthur Hailey
☐ AIRPORT 37½p (7/6)
☐ IN HIGH PLACES 30p (6/–)

Georgette Heyer

☐ SYLVESTER 30p (6/–)
☐ BATH TANGLE 25p (5/–)
☐ BLACK SHEEP 25p (5/–)

Robin Maugham

☐ THE SECOND WINDOW 35p (7/–)

James Barlow

☐ THE BURDEN OF PROOF 30p (6/–)

Catherine Marshall

☐ CHRISTY 37½p (7/6)

Grace Metalious

☐ RETURN TO PEYTON PLACE 17½p (3/6)
☐ NO ADAM IN EDEN 17½p (3/6)

Nicholas Monsarrat

☐ RICHER THAN ALL HIS TRIBE 35p (7/–)

Norman Collins

☐ THE GOVERNOR'S LADY 40p (8/–)

Kyle Onstott

☐ MANDINGO 30p (6/–)
☐ DRUM 35p (7/–)
☐ MASTER OF FALCONHURST 35p (7/–)

Kyle Onstott and Lance Horner

☐ FALCONHURST FANCY 30p (6/–)

Lance Horner

☐ THE MUSTEE 35p (7/–)

Jean Plaidy

☐ THE MURDER IN THE TOWER 30p (6/–)
☐ THE THISTLE AND THE ROSE 30p (6/–)
☐ THE GOLDSMITH'S WIFE 30p (6/–)
☐ THE SPANISH BRIDEGROOM 30p (6/–)
☐ THE WANDERING PRINCE 25p (5/–)
☐ A HEALTH UNTO HIS MAJESTY 25p (5/–)
☐ HERE LIES OUR SOVEREIGN LORD 25p (5/–)

Nevil Shute

☐ NO HIGHWAY 25p (5/–)
☐ THE CHEQUER BOARD 25p (5/–)
☐ TRUSTEE FROM THE TOOLROOM 25p (5/–)
☐ A TOWN LIKE ALICE 25p (5/–)

Alan Sillitoe

☐ SATURDAY NIGHT AND SUNDAY MORNING 20p (4/–)
☐ GUZMAN, GO HOME 25p (5/–)

Wilbur Smith

☐ THE SOUND OF THUNDER 30p (6/–)